Coconut

Coconut

Kopano Matlwa

JACANA

First published by Jacana Media (Pty) Ltd in 2007

10 Orange Street
Sunnyside
Auckland Park 2092
South Africa
+2711 628 3200
www.jacana.co.za

ISBN 978-1-77009-336-2

Set in Sabon 11/14
Printed by CTP Book Printers, Cape Town
Job No. 000435

See a complete list of Jacana titles at www.jacana.co.za

Dedicated to you, child of my country

Oh goodness, oh my, I cannot believe this has happened, is happening, and that you, my dearest Coconut, are now real. Thank you, Lord! I cannot believe you, you are so sneaky; who would have guessed you had this planned all along! Mama and Papa, what and where would I be without you? You are my greatest teachers and my bestest friends, the most inspiring two people I know. Thank God I was born a Matlwa. J. Tumelo, my sister, my confidante, partner in crime and trusty editor, you've been so patient with me, your big sister who so often acts like your little one. Thank you for never tiring of my dramas and always having an ear to listen. Monewa, my favouritest brother in the world, your prayers and your hugs kept me going. The Kekanas and the Matlwas, all my grannies, grandpas, uncles and aunts, you all sacrificed so much for us, your children. Thank you, we owe all we have to you. Motlatsi, for your love, for being my pillar and strength, I don't know how you put up with me, thank you and 458. And last but not least, my dear friend Mampho Motjidibane Bapela, I do not have the words to thank you enough; you believed in Coconut from the very beginning, and urged me on when I tired of trying. Can you believe it?

Kopano Matlwa

Part One

In a pew on the right, a couple of rows ahead of mine, sits a tiny chocolate girl. Her scraggy neck and jabbing elbows make me think of sticky chicken wings served with Sunday lunch. The sermon is not particularly riveting so I am easily distracted by anything that is willing. Braids: plastic, shiny, cheap synthetic strands of dreams-come-true make their way out from her underaged head. Sponono, in a burdensomely layered satin floral dress, sits silently beside her mother, running her fingers through the knotted mess of a little girl's desires. An old and tattered woollen hair-band makes shapes of eight into and out of the blackness. Over and over again it goes, gawky arms moving almost rhythmically, juxtaposing greedy fingers.

Kate Jones had the most beautiful hair I had ever seen in all my eight years of life. Burnt amber. Autumn leaves. The setting sun. Her heavy and soft hair, curled slightly at its ends, would make proud swishes as she rolled around the playground.

Kate was overfed and hoggish. Kate was spoilt and haughty. Kate was rude and foul-mouthed. But with that hair, Kate was glorious. Dazzled by its radiance, class teachers overlooked the red crosses in Kate's school workbooks, monstrous bullies exempted Kate from the pushing and prodding that all the juniors endured, popular kids made no fun of Kate's podgy face and swollen ankles, and little black girls scattered helter-skelter, doing her favours in return for a feel of her hair.

I still do not know whether it was earnest, malicious, or out of some sort of contorted curiosity but Kate asked

1

me one day, during Music, if I could plait her hair into thin plaits like the braids that adorned my head. She said my braids were pretty and that she wished she could have hair just like mine so she could be as beautiful as I was. Flabbergasted, I smiled a very broad smile, endeavouring to process the words. I immediately got to work, little hands moving swiftly, but not too swiftly, careful to make every one look exact.

The bell rang. Kate abruptly stood up to leave, and then caught her reflection.

But I was not finished yet!

First tears, then heads turning, then silence, then more tears, then shouting.
"My hair!"
But I am not finished yet!
"What is the matter, dear Kate?"
But Mrs Reed, I am not finished yet!
"My hair!"
"Fifi, what have you done?"
Please Mrs Reed, I am not finished yet!
"My hair!"
"Fifi, you insolent child, what have you done to Kate's hair?"
"My hair!"
Please Kate, let me just finish, then you will see!
"Fifi T, answer me! What have you done?"
"Take it out, take it out, take it out now!"

Something that the preacher says momentarily gets me stuck in the sermon again but my mind soon wriggles back out. My little chocolate distraction, now frustrated with the inept woollen hair-band, yanks it forcefully out of her hair. She flinches. The hair-band falls to the ground, landing at her mother's feet. Entangled in the hair-band is a long black braid with a tuft of hair at its end. Sponono sees it and begins to cry. The choir ladies are not happy. They rotate their necks around their curved backs and look first at Sponono, then at her mother and then at Sponono again. Sponono continues to cry. When the choir ladies begin to shift uncomfortably in their seats, Sponono's mother, finding no other solution to the problem, picks up her handbag, the braid (still entangled in the woollen hair-band) and Sponono, and they all leave together.

Pain is beauty, grandmother used to say. Well, not *my* grandmother, but I am certain *somebody's* grandmother used to say that, and if my grandmother cared for such, I am sure she would say it too.

Ous Beauty would seat me on a high stool, so I could swing my legs while I waited for her to finish washing, blowing, dyeing, cutting, permming and styling her other customer's hair. Month End was always a frantic time at Ous Beauty's, because at Month End everybody felt rich. In the drawer at the level of my knees Ous Beauty kept a comb with the finest of teeth. In the mirror in front of me sat a girl with the coarsest of hair. That the two could work in harmony, I would never be convinced. Such pain. Teeth gritted, I watched her artificial red nails part my wiry hair so that she could base my scalp with Vitamin, Shea Butter and Lanolin Hair Food. I held my breath at every pull and attempted to concentrate on the snap of the gum she chewed so explicitly. I knew that by now the palms of my hands were an unbearable shade of red, from digging my nails in too deep. I hid them under a ten-year-old bottom, and shut my eyes tight, refusing to let out the tears that wrestled violently within. The Black Queen hair-straightener cream could be smelt long before it was seen. The black American TV girls on the box of the relaxer cream had hair so straight and so long that Mama assured me it could not be real. Ous Beauty then began to smear the cream on my hair. I always watched her vigilantly, making sure she did not miss a spot. A chemical reaction. A painful exothermic chemical reaction. Burn. Burning. Burnt. When Ous Beauty asked me if I was ready to wash it out, I said no. I wanted every last tiny weenie curl straight.

In the mirror I watched the fine-toothed comb slip effortlessly through my silky soft and straight Black Queen hair. I was not bothered by the tenderness of my scalp that sent quivers down my neck as the teeth of the comb slid past it, nor was I alarmed at the white of my roots that had come to the surface. No, I was just delighted to be beautiful again.

The upper half of the walls of our church are made completely of glass. The glass is brightly coloured into images of the saints and is so chunky that when you try to look through it, people on the exterior take on distorted forms. I imagine there are a lot of saints, so I am sure it is not all of them that I see gazing at us from the walls of the church. Our church is named after St. Francis of Assisi. I heard or read somewhere that St. Francis was once a most fashionable, wild and wealthy, reckless young man, celebrated amongst the youth of Assisi. He gave it all up to live a life of simplicity and so peaceful and humble did he become that the birds would come rest on his shoulders while he prayed.

In summer the sun shines through the glass of saints, and beams of colour, carrying tiny particles of what looks magical, but is probably just dust, meet at the centre of the aisle. When I was younger I used to think that those tiny particles descended every Sunday to protect the congregation from the evils of the world outside.

"Say it, Tshepo, just say it."
"I don't know, Ofilwe, it's just…"
"It's just what, Tshepo? Why can you not just say what is on your mind? Speak!"
"It is like advertising. You market a product well enough and anybody will buy it."
"Christianity, a product? Lord, are you listening to this? Are you crazy, Tshepo? Our whole social system is built on Christianity: our calendar, holidays, laws. Our upbringing. Now you want to tell me that it is all one big scam?"
"All I am saying is that my skin is black."
"No. Don't you dare try to take this away from me too. I am not going to apologise for my beliefs for your Africanism.
"It is not Africanism."
"Then what is it?"

5

Our family of four – Mama, Daddy, Tshepo and I – has been coming to St. Francis Anglican Church ever since we moved from a vaguely remembered Mabopane to Little Valley Country Estate. Our new home was closer to my father's Sandton City offices and Tshepo's preparatory school. I was to begin nursery school that year and Tshepo grade one, although he should have been in grade two but was held back a year, because he did not speak English as well as his new, elite, all-boys' school would have liked.

We commence to sing the Peace Song. The Presentation of the Gifts and the Holy Eucharist follow. I know the proceedings so well that I am certain I could take the service if I so desired. I ceased using the prayer book in grade six when I realised that I knew all the congregation's responses by heart. When Tshepo used to come to church with us we would say the priest's part too, to see who knew it best.

Dear Diary
27 September 1997

Tomorrow is the 28th of September, the day of Tim Browning's sleep-over party. I'm sure they will all be dancing the night away, while I sit in the middle of nowhere doing a whole bunch of fat nothing. Mama says I can't go. Typical.

Nothing in my life is of any importance to anyone in this house. I just don't understand them. How can they do this to me? I asked Daddy if I could go the same day I got the invitation and he said yes. The whole day at school yesterday, everybody was talking about what they would be wearing to the party. For the first time in a long while I could actually take part in the conversations, because for the first time in a long while I was actually going to a real party and not the stupid grade-one-type jumping castle parties that my dumb friends throw. Well, that's what I thought anyway.

Mama tells me in the car, on our way home yesterday, that a former Headmaster of Thuto Pele Primary School in Atteridgeville was shot last weekend by two men he gave a lift to. She says he is married and that their youngest child is twelve, just as old as I am. She says that we are leaving for the funeral tomorrow morning (the 28th of September!) and that I should tell Tshepo that both of us need to be in bed early because we need to be out of the house by 5am sharp.

That's when I blew. How could they forget about the biggest event of the year? Or do they just not care? They are trying to destroy my life. I'm sure of it! Look, don't get me wrong, I feel really sorry for the man and his family. I don't want to even think about life without Daddy. But what difference will me being there make? The people don't even know me. What will they care?

My mother tells me, "It is respect, Ofilwe. Maybe she not know you or even me very very good. But these things we must do. We must be there at the funeral. Hmm? All of us must be there. These things are of immense importance. Very very great importance. We appreciate each other. We support each other. Next

7

thing it is misfortune on our family. Huh? Just think about that. Also us, we will need these people."

Bla dee bla dee bla fishpaste! I shot back, "Not actually, Mama, I do not want a bunch of strangers at my funeral pretending to care when all they are there for is the food!"

No, I didn't say that. I thought it, though, and probably should have said it. It's high time Mama knows how I feel. Doesn't she understand that this party is my big chance? Tim Browning doesn't just invite anybody to his parties. He wants me there for a reason. He told me once that I was different. Tim said that I was not like the other black girls in our class. He said I was calmer, cuter and that I looked a little like Scary Spice.

At nuptial and burial ceremonies, at thanksgiving days *ge re phasa Badimo*, I stand in reverence, out of everybody's way, silently taking it all in, feeling most inadequate amongst a group of people who all seem to know exactly what roles they play in the age-old Pedi rituals. As the only female grandchild, I fear that day when my turn comes to run these sacred occasions. Organise, arrange, coordinate, sort out, control, fix... Speak! What is it that one is supposed to say? Perhaps there was a class I missed, lessons in my youth that I was supposed to attend and for some unexplored reason did not. I do not know what the mourning woman should wear, which way her yellow mattress should face, how long she should dress in black for, pray for, kneel for, cry for. I do not know who to call or who to send. What now if I command the guests to sing before the rain has fallen or beckon the children to sit on the left at the back instead of in the front on the side? I do not know how the sensitive messages are relayed, whether it is too soon or getting too late. I do not know how I am supposed to know, and whether I will ever know.

"Mama, what did we believe in before the missionaries came?"
"Badimo."
"Badimo?"
"Yes, Ofilwe, Badimo."
"Badimo and what else? What else did we believe Mama?"
"Just Badimo, Ofilwe."
"But surely we had our own traditional rites, a name for our God, a form of worship? Whatever happened to that?"
"I do not know, Ofilwe."
"Tshepo says they, the missionaries, tricked us Mama. Or doesn't it matter?"
"No. It does not matter, Ofilwe."
"Do you think bo Koko would know?"
"Maybe, Ofilwe."
"Or was it before their time? When did the missionaries come?"
" I do not know, Ofilwe. Goodnight."
"OK, Mama, goodnight."

I attend this ancient church because I am comfortable here. I understand nothing of the history of the church. I do not know what the word 'Anglican' means nor can I explain to you how the church came to arise. It is simple. I come here because I feel I belong. That is all. The traditions of the church are my own. I do not have any others.

After the service we follow our shadows down the white stony path to where our car is parked. In the days when there were four shadows, I used to watch them as they awkwardly moved ahead of us, sometimes catching them looking back to see if we were still behind them. I wondered how they knew where we wanted to go. In the days when there were four of them, Tshepo's long and gangly shadow would glide ahead of all of ours as Tshepo ran to secure the front seat. Every Sunday Mama would futilely try to beat Tshepo to it and then scold him for taking her seat when her high heels and years prevented her from getting there before him. Every Sunday Daddy would remind Tshepo that in car accidents the passenger in the front seat is always the worst hit. Every Sunday Tshepo would smugly buckle up and pretend that he could not hear either of them.

After the 9.30am Family Service, all members of our church are invited to juice and biscuits in the hall-cum-school-cum-gymnasium across from the chapel. Even though it is seldom both juice and biscuits that the tea ladies provide, I often wish that we could stay. Watching our shadows lead us away from the soaring walls of the church and to our car as they have done every Sunday since I can remember, I realise that with age I have come to accept my family of four just the way it is. Mama is amiable but has no time to get too involved in the happenings of St. Francis Anglican Church. And Daddy – well, Daddy plays golf.

I didn't tell Tshepo because I knew that he would believe me. I needed somebody to convince me that

11

I was lying. You see, the problem with Tshepo is that he thinks too much. Tshepo and Daddy had not been getting along very well and I didn't want to exacerbate the tension between them.

I swear. It happened innocently. I do not pry. I would have been better off not knowing (whatever it is I think I now know). I needed to urgently call Maritza so that we could plan whether it would be wiser to dress in pants or skirts for school the next day, but Mama had been hogging the phone. I was getting anxious because it was getting late and Maritza's parents did not take kindly to calls coming in after eight.

I discreetly picked up the study-room phone and used my pyjama top to cover the voice-piece. I wanted to know why Mama was still on the line. She was crying. Mama never cries. Koko was on the other end, which is not anything out of the ordinary because Mama and her mother speak daily. However, this conversation was different. Koko was speaking softly and so sternly with Mama. Koko said that Mama needed to stop acting like a spoilt child. Koko said that John – Daddy – was a man and that men do these things with other women, but that it does not mean he does not care for Mama. Koko said that Mama lives a life that many women from where she comes from can only dream of and that she cannot jeopardise that by 'this crazy talk of divorce'.

"Divorce? You must never. Do not be selfish, Gemina. You must think, my child. Think. Use your head. Huh, Gemina? Have you forgotten your responsibilities,

Gemina? You have two young children... you must for them care. Two. Where do you think you will go if you leave John? Back home? Where, Gemina? Where do you have to go? What will become of all of you? Huh? Nothing. Without him, my girl, you is nothing."

Nothing. Such a strong word. Nothing. I wondered about many things after Koko put down the phone and Mama walked up the stairs to slam her bedroom door. Was Koko right? Would I have turned out to be nothing if Mama had not married Daddy? Would I not be the same Ofilwe I am now if Mama had never made it out of the dreaded location? What if Mama had chosen love, where would I be now? What would I be now? Nothing?

Instead of waking up to my cubed fruit, muesli and mixed nuts on a bed of low-fat granadilla yoghurt, would I begin my day by polishing the red stoep that juts out at the front of Koko's two-roomed house? When bored, would I pass the time by naming stones and creating homes for them in the wet dirt that surrounds Koko's self-made outside toilet instead of playing Solitaire on Mama's laptop, as I do now? Would I steal handfuls of sugar from the former mielie-meal bucket under the sink and run out to lie on the grass to let the sweet crystals melt on my tongue instead of forgetting to give Daddy back his change, forget it was not mine for the keeping and forget I was not supposed to use it to buy honey and almond nougat bars from the health shop outside the estate gates. Instead of a decaf Café Latte at Bedazzle on

13

Thursday nights would I freeze my Cool-Aid and save it for a really hot day? Would it matter to me who my clothes were named after?

Would I go into respiratory distress at the thought of wearing garments with no names at all? Would it be the complex security guard's wandering eye or gunshots drawing ever closer in the night that made me uneasy? Would it be brightly lit tarred roads or whistling dusty streets that I travelled along?

As we climb into the car, there is a loud crashing sound that comes from the hall-cum-school-cum-gymnasium across from the chapel. A sound like cutlery, crockery, jars of jam and empty ice-cream tubs sliding off high shelves and crashing, smashing, shattering and thumping onto the floor... and some people's heads. It gives all of us a fright and Daddy drops the car keys under the seat. A roar of laughter from the hall-cum-school-cum-gymnasium follows the loud crashing sound. It is obviously nothing serious.

"Where were you born, Fifi?"
"In Johannesburg, Mrs Williamson."
"Don't lie, Ofilwe, you were born in a stinky shack!"
"No I wasn't, Zama! Shut up."
"Stop being nasty, Zama. Fifi was not born in any sort of shack, were you, Fifi?"
"No, Mrs Williamson."

Our ageing car jitters slightly, sending tingles up my spine, as we drive on the gravel, out of the chalky churchyard, into the black road. Today I sit in the back seat alone. Mama sits in the front, alongside Daddy. Tshepo is at home, most likely lying in the hammock he claimed as his own when we discovered it at the bottom of the garden in our playing days. At one stage in my life my body was just short enough to fit along the length of the backseat. However, I never had it to myself then, so could never enjoy the luxury of using its cream hide as a bed when my eyes tired of watching trees flash past the window. Besides being far too tall and far too old for that now, I am no longer exhilarated by the idea of spreading my body across the back of Daddy's car.

Stuart Simons is an obnoxious pig. What does he know about my family? I was so excited for Daddy. He had yearned for this specific car for almost a year, and could now finally afford it. Before the car came, Daddy used to page longingly through the automobile magazines and point out that in that specific car he would have 'all the right machinery to roll with the big dogs'. Daddy would pick me up and put me on his shoulders and whisper that in that specific car he would cut all the right deals for sure, and with all the money he would make he would buy his precious Ofilwe all the chocolate-covered gobstoppers her heart desired. We had all gone to help him choose a colour, and had agreed that a silver-grey suited that specific car best.

Daddy never fetches me from school, so when Mama was away staying at Ous Matilda's, who had just given birth, I had told just about everybody who cared to listen that my Daddy was picking me up in his new Mercedes-Benz.

But when Daddy finally does arrive, I am no longer standing outside the towering rusty school gates with all my friends and a few nosy others. Instead, I am sitting on the grass mound playing five-cards with the ice-cream man, who is the only interesting company there is left. As I am getting up, Stuart Simons walks from the high-school sport fields towards the parking lot with a clique of senior boys who I know are only allowing Stuart to hang with them because he is wealthy. Although I have never liked Stuart very much, I wave bye to him so that he can see me climbing into the most captivating car on the school grounds. As I open the boot to put my bag in, Stuart walks over and says something like "Nice wheels, Ofilwe, who did your father hijack this one from?"

I want to smash his skull in with the cricket bat he is holding in his hand and watch the red blood trickle down his freckled face. Instead, I slam the boot shut, fling the silver-grey front door open, and scream at Daddy for picking me up late.

There is a vintage jet-black lady who sells ready-to-eat *Maotoana* at the notorious Schubert intersection. She is there every Sunday, so as we near those crossroads, I sit up to see if I can spot her before we speed past the green light. Unlike the other street vendors who periodically jive in between the cars, pressing their noses against electronic windows, psychedelic products in hand, toothless smiles searching for the rare interested individual, Makhulu sits motionless underneath her generous orange umbrella, waiting for us to come to her. Makhulu has been operating at this

16

intersection for just over two months now, but already she seems to own it. Her leathery skin, folded into a hundred-and-two deep lines, makes it difficult for one to read emotion off her face. Her bold bead-like eyes stare straight ahead, suggesting a mind preoccupied. Her chin is always slightly raised, her back strikingly straight for someone her age and her hands are always neatly placed in her lap. I secretly believe that Makhulu is of royal blood.

On days when the spray-painted traffic lights do grant me an opportunity to observe the business of street vending outside our centrally locked doors, I see the teenage newspaper boy bring Makhulu a one-litre glass Coke bottle filled with water to drink. The raucous 'ID-book-cover and hands-free-kit for sale' twin brothers drop their heads and cup their hands together as a greeting every time they pass by Makhulu's throne. Each time we stop, I make an attempt to catch her eye. I never manage to and do not know what I would do if I ever did.

Grandmother Tlou, Daddy's mother, can tell you anything, including the things nobody would bother to know, about the British royal family. Grandmother Tlou took a week off from work at the Department of Education after she had heard the news of the sudden death of Diana, Princess of Wales. Aunty Sophia, Daddy's verbose cousin who was raised by Grandmother Tlou and Grandfather Tlou because Grandfather Tlou owned a butchery in Atteridgeville and could afford to do so, called Daddy to report what was going on at the face-brick Atteridgeville Gardens

17

house. Grandmother Tlou apparently announced that she would no longer be attending meals for the next three days as a sign of respect for the passing of the great princess. Aunty Sophia later told Tshepo, after the tension around Grandmother Tlou's condition had subsided, that after her announcement Grandmother Tlou commenced packing away all her clothing of colour, including her trademark Emporium scarves, into the spare bedroom downstairs, committing herself to dress in black until such a time when it would be appropriate to cease mourning. Although Daddy chided Grandmother Tlou for appearing to be more devastated over the death of the princess than that of her own husband four years earlier, he returned from a business trip in London with 18-ct white-gold loop earrings similar to those that Diana once wore, in an attempt to ease Grandmother's suffering.

Who is my own Princess Di? Does my royal family still exist, some place out there in barren, rural South Africa? Please, do tell me about their dynasty. I am afraid my history only goes as far back as lessons on the Dutch East India Company in grade two at Laerskool Valley Primary School. Were they once a grand people, ruling over a mighty nation, audaciously fighting off the advance of the colourless ones? Do you perhaps know where they are now?

I have heard some hiss that the heirs to their thrones sit with swollen bellies and emaciated limbs under a merciless sun, waiting for government grants. Surely that cannot be true.

As we cross the intersection, having fulfilled our Sunday obligation, leaving guilt behind and driving back into the secular, I wonder what my own family will be like. Unlike some of my female friends, I do not have a picture of an ideal husband in mind nor am I certain whether I even fancy one.

Strangely enough, I think about my future children quite a bit. I imagine lovely round dimpled faces and Colgate smiles running past sticky walls. In my dreams they are painted in shades of pink. I am afraid of what that means.

Little Square Shopping Centre is where the important people of Little Valley prefer to do their buying. Mama comes here every day of the week to purchase the food she will prepare for our evening meal. I am absolutely certain Mama is perfectly aware that in an age of cute baby-blue freezers and touch-screen microwaves it is completely unnecessary to shop daily. I have now stopped trying to draw this to her attention and have accepted it as another one of Mama's peculiar indulgences. Sundays are the only days I come here willingly, because on Sundays after church we, the Tlou family, have breakfast at Silver Spoon Coffee Shop.

Today, unlike other days, Fikile is our waitress. She shows us to the only remaining table, thoughtlessly placed threateningly close to the swinging kitchen doors. Silver Spoon is a small establishment and Fikile and Ayanda are the only waiters who work here.

19

I do not like Fikile. She has a strange air about her. Although small, Silver Spoon is fashionable and its customers are loyal. Besides Tshepo, who insists that nothing compares to a bowl of soft-pap porridge prepared by our domestic worker Old Virginia, our family worships Silver Spoon's Traditional English Breakfast. So we, too, are loyal. Fikile usually serves the other customers because they ask for her, and Ayanda serves us. I personally prefer it that way, and I am confident she does too. Although I am surprised Ayanda is not serving us today, I say nothing for fear of Fikile spitting in our food. I would not put it past her.

"Tshepo my darly! Tshepo-wee, tell your sister to come quick inside, our guests is come."

I can hear Mama from where I am, but carry on making headstands in the pool. I am not ready to get out yet, the water's warm and I still need to work on my back-flips. Mama always-always chooses the times when I am having fun to send me around. I see Tshepo coming out of the house and quickly sink under water.

"Ofilwe, stop being stupid. I can see you under there and I know you can hear me. Get out and come greet Mama's guests."

I don't understand why the people in this house can't just leave me alone. Mama and her guests drive everybody crazy. This is probably why Daddy spends all his weekends at Golf City. As I enter the living room, Tshepo brings in a tray of sultana grapes, salted crackers, cheese wedges, carrot and celery sticks, and honey mustard pretzels for the ladies I recognise as the nursing sisters Mama used to work with.

"Oooo! Here she is. Ofilwe, you are wet! Oh, Ofilwe. My floor. What a mess. Bona, Ofilwe! Be careful, man. Hayi. These children! Ofilwe, do you still remember Mama Solly le Mama Katlego? Come, come. It's a long time since they see you last, isn't it? Come greet them nicely."

"Hi."

I don't understand why the people in this house can't just leave me alone! I was minding my own business when Tshepo dragged me out of the pool to come greet Mama's guests, and then when I did exactly that, Mama looked at me in horror as if I had sworn at them. What on earth is wrong with the word 'Hi'? Everybody says 'Hi'.

Later, she'd complain to my grandmother. "It is a great embarrassing, Koko. Hayi! You should have been here to hear your little Ofilwe. Those women are my elders, not even I would speak with them in such a manner. 'Hi'. Just like that, Koko. 'Hi'. As if. You'd think she's doing them a favour by greeting them. Is a simple 'Dumelang bo Mama' too much to ask? It's not right, Koko. No, it is not right one bit. What kind of children am I raising?"

I know that Fikile knows that we do not need this much time to decide on what it is we are going to eat.

I know that Fikile knows that we order the same Silver Spoon's Traditional English Breakfast every Sunday, without exception. I know that Fikile is not as busy as she is pretending to be. She stands with her right hand on her hip and her left in her hair at a table of three blue-eyed males, all of whom look at least forty years her senior. Two of them appear to be somewhat drunk, speaking too loudly for the proximity of their chairs. The third man is conversing with Fikile. She seems pleased with the things he is saying to her. Fikile shakes her head in false disapproval and laughs shrilly as she walks away from the table. She looks straight through me.

Fikile can't be much older than me. Is she not embarrassed? Does she not wonder what the rest of us will think of her Hanky-Pankies with that *Oupa*? The grey-haired, pale man with the blue eyes she has been speaking to looks like he has been in that suit since Friday morning. Stale. The type you know is pathetically desperate. *Sies*. Is a lack of melanin her only criterion?

Junior P. Mokoena used to head the table next to mine in the third term of grade seven at Laerskool Valley Primary School. Mrs van Niekerk, my red and round grade seven mathematics teacher, arranged her class in such a way that the top six grade seven pupils would each head their own table of four pupils. Mrs van Niekerk changed the table arrangement of pupils after every class test and said that in this way the stronger pupils in the class could help the not-so-strong pupils and that some day we would all be as equally strong.

Shame. Mrs van Niekerk was a sweet lady, but perhaps a little naive. Her table system became a fierce competition amongst the top students in the class to see who could head the most number of tables each term while the not-so-strong students remained not so strong.

Junior P. Mokoena always got the highest marks in our mathematics class tests and as a result was never moved from his table, a grave, deep-brown table that became known as Junior's Table. In the third term of that year I was, for the first time ever in my life, in the top six of the grade seven mathematics class. Mrs van Niekerk, as I had so desperately hoped, assigned me to head the table next to Junior's. I remember slowly packing my yellow space-case into my matching single-strap, over-the-shoulder Mall Rat bag, and walking over to my prize as if it was as inconsequential as the sentiments of the not-so-strong pupils I was leaving behind. Honestly, being in the top six had never been a key priority of mine. I had worked hard for this class test because I knew that it was the only way I would ever get Junior P. Mokoena to recognise me.

I hated Junior. I hated how he walked around the school as if all and sundry wanted to be him. I hated that they actually did. I thought it moronic that he was the topic of our every conversation. I did not care that he had his own driver or that their indoor swimming pool was Olympic size. It did not matter to me that his mother was one of the first black female neurosurgeons in the country and that his father owned all the bottlestores in Soweto. Who cares if the

Mokoenas are spending the festive season in Spain? I did not ask for daily updates on Junior P. Mokoena's glamorous life and I was tired of getting them.

"Tell her that I only date white girls."

I do not remember feeling sad at the words, just rage. Anger at myself for being so foolish, contempt towards the love letter I had written which still lay open on his arrogant desk for all his fans to see, and hatred for the boy that had just ruined my life. Who did Junior P. Mokoena think he was?

"Hi. My name is Fikile. Are you ready to order?"

Ayanda and Fikile dress in black jeans and a black T-shirt with a print of a large silver spoon running down their spines. If it were not for the white aprons they tie around their waists and the darting they have to do from table to table and for the fact that, besides us and the kitchen staff, they are the only black people in Silver Spoon, you could mistake them for customers. They blend in far better than Tshepo does in his yellow rooster suit which he wears to make deliveries for Instant Fried Chicken in Pine Slopes. Tshepo started working there when I was in grade eight and he was in grade eleven, first as a waiter then as a delivery boy.

When Tshepo told me he had inquired about a waitering job at Instant Fried Chicken, a greasy little fast-food joint in Pine Slopes, I laughed because I did not think he was serious. As much as Tshepo liked to push the whole "down with the people thing", he is by nature the type whose mere existence depends on being intellectually stimulated, so I was pretty certain that even if he was to go as far as showing up for his first day at work, he wouldn't last longer than a week.

Of course there's no use in trying to reason with Tshepo when he's made up his mind, so when the day came for Tshepo to go in to work I simply waved goodbye and went back to sleep. I don't think I even asked how it went when he got back later that afternoon because I knew he would lie. "It was great," he told Mama at supper that evening. Lies. How could it be great? How can cleaning after people ever be great? He exasperated me, Tshepo, so I ignored the whole thing, and if we spoke at all we spoke about other stuff and not his dumb job.

But a couple of months later while rummaging in his room for a sharpener, I came across what may have been an entry in his journal.

I realise when I get there that Mama, as I had quietly suspected, was wrong about the traffic. I arrive at 6.15, forty-five minutes early, to an abandoned parking lot. There are no cars going towards Pine Slopes on that road at that time of the morning. I initially park right outside Instant Fried Chicken. There is a 'Staff Only' sign back there, but I decide that parking there would appear somewhat forward. So I park in the open parking area, close to Ashanti's, the boutique where Mama buys her hair.

Isabella, the lady I sent the email to, is not there as we arranged, but there is a closed Indian man involved with the till, who says, once hesitantly asked, that he is Sir Nathan, the manager, and that Isabella has told him nothing about anything. Nevertheless he writes "Tshepo Tlou" on a name tag which he sticks on my shirt and points me to the kitchen and recommends that I make myself 'visibly useful' until Isabella arrives.

It is eerie being here without the customers. I battle to find my bearings. The three-legged, glow-in-the-dark, lime-and-orange stools, packed face down along the length of the tables, look like simple-minded mutant recruits under the 6.17am Monday morning light. The door I think leads to the kitchen is locked, so I stand ready outside it. I hear them before I see them. The group of men and women, singing Mafikizolo's "We bhuti ndihamba nawe", carrying black-and-yellow chequered plastic bags which hold empty skaftiens that will later be filled with customer's leftovers, are the Instant Fried Chicken staff. I am afraid of them. I know I am different. I reek of KTV, IEB, MTV and ICC, although I have tried to mask it behind All Stars sneakers and a free Youth League election T-shirt. I am certain they will catch me out as soon as I open my mouth. They do not, or rather, if they do, it is of no significance, for they treat me like any other. I too stand above the deep buckets of fierce oil: plucking, washing, stuffing, spicing, basting, turning one naked chicken after the other, but not managing to sing 'ndihamba nawe' simultaneously, like the rest of the staff promise.

The faceless Isabella does ultimately arrive. The room temperature plummets. I feel her before I see her. The chorus comes to an abrupt halt, just as we are getting to 'We bhuti!' Sepekere spots Isabella's TT pulling into the 'Staff Only' space I am now grateful I did not park in. Sis Giant, attempting to jump off the counter and throw her coffee down the sink at the same time, causes everything around her to vibrate violently. Poor Pinki drops a tray of breasts into the searing oil. Sir Nathan yells from the floor that we are moving too slowly and Small mutters that I should pick up a knife, fast. She enters with a 'tah-dah', dressed from head to toe in pink. Her olive skin, unusual green eyes and dark brown locks suggest she is from across the equator, towards the left.

She is irritated. She screams in an unfamiliar accent, that Table No. 5 asked for Lemon and Herb but that we gave them Schwit Chilli. Schwit Chilli? She asks us, between profanities, why it is that we have difficulty distinguishing between the two, and whether it is because we only have a crèche-school level education. I am offended. I must correct her, point out that I, Tshepo Tlou, in fact graduated as Dux Scholar from my junior school, taking all the subject prizes including The Reader Award and the certificate for Most Promising Pupil from an Underprivileged Background. She will curl up in shame when she hears I have received academic honours three years in succession at my current high school, am Vice-Captain of the senior cricket team despite my age, co-chair of the debating society, deputy president of Student Link and have just recently been offered a scholarship to further my education at any tertiary institution in the country. I, however, dare not utter a word, it is still early, I must be patient, there will come a time when I will educate this woman.

Isabella puts me to work on the floor, not before reminding me that she is doing me a great service by hiring me because 'already, I am overstaffed'. She does not normally do this, she adds, so I must not forget that I am very fortunate. She commends me for my politeness and says she hopes I will teach her air-headed staff a thing or two about manners. She sighs heavily. 'We must try do a part to help with the unemployment in this country.' She sighs again, says, 'Even if you employing lazy, ungrateful people who don't deserve nothing.' The sigh that follows this last statement is drawn out and smells of garlic. There is silence and I am uncertain if it is my prompt to say something. Say what? Should I congratulate her? I try a 'you are a good woman, ma'am.' She shrugs. She smiles. This time I sigh, relieved that I am in the door. However, my hallelujahs are cut short by a sharp 'Enough talking. This restaurant does not run itself.' I am to wait on Section B with Nozipho, a charming jelly-tot of a waitress with cornrows.

I squeeze between the tables, not noticing the full-faced purple-nosed housewife who sits hunched up like a beach ball at the table on my right. She looks up. Our eyes meet or at least I think they do. 'Good morning ma'am,' I genially greet, picking up the salt cellar I am sure she does not know has dropped off her table. Does she not hear me? Perhaps she has a great

28

deal on her mind. That look, or rather lack thereof, sticks with me throughout the day, maybe because it is foreign or maybe because it is one I get over and over again as I move from one table of milky faces to another. Do these people not see me, hear me, when I speak to them? Why do they look through me as if I do not exist, click their fingers at me as if it is the only language I understand?

I am enraged. I want to call them all to order. Tell them that they have no right treating people the way they do. I want them to hear my voice. I want them to listen to the manner in which I speak. I want to slap their stuffed faces with my private school articulation and hurl their empty skulls into a dizzy spin with the diction I use. I will quote our democratic Constitution. I will remind them that it is now, and not then. I will demand respect.

I purposefully stride into the kitchen certain that the staff will agree with me on my decision to raise this matter with Isabella urgently. Surely we cannot be expected to graciously serve such offensive people? The staff, however, do not share my passion; instead they ridicule it.

'It is true!' they chuckle, without even looking up from the plucking, washing, stuffing, spicing, basting, and turning of Lemon and Herbs and Schwit Chillis. 'These Model C children know nothing of the real world. They are shocked by the ways of Umlungu. *It is good you have come to work, boy. There is much you must learn.'*

29

Now that lunch hour is over, the singing begins again, except this time the kitchen's song is a wordless hum. Isabella is still in the building. I am ashamed. I sit outside under the insensitive three o'clock sun, with a menu hanging from my hand, pretending to memorise the items. Small, who brags that he is the only waiter to have ever scored 100% in the Instant Fried Chicken menu test, sleeps a bottomless sleep on the step below me after having been annoyed by the ease at which I learnt the names of the dishes. I do not know why I am there. I do not need the money nor will the experience be of use to me in any of my desired career paths. I deplore the customers. I despise Isabella. I detest what the kitchen represents. I do not know what I am trying to prove, why I must prove it and to whom.

We are regulars here at Silver Spoon, but are not chummy with Miss Becky, the owner, like the other regulars are. I am familiar with most of the beaming faces in here today, but do not jump up excitedly when I see any of them enter nor do I blow darling kisses across tables as they often do when they see each other.

Fikile, we all agree, fits in fine. It is our fault that after numerous breakfasts, one Sunday morning after another, we have not tried to assimilate ourselves into the Silver Spoon Coffee Shop family tree.

I hate it, Lord. I hate it with every atom of my heart. I am angry, Lord. I am searing within. I am furious. I do not understand. Why, Lord? Look at us, Lord, sitting in this corner. A corner. A hole. Daddy believes he enjoys this food. Poor Mama, she still struggles with this fork and knife thing. Poor us. Poor, poor, poor pathetic us. It is pitiful. What are we doing here? Why did we come? We do not belong.

Lord, I am cross with You. I, they, thousands of us, devote our lives to You. Some, Father, labouring endlessly so that You may be pleased. But still, Lord, still we are shackled. Some shackled around the ankles and wrists, others around their hearts, but most, Lord, are shackled around their minds.

They laugh nastily, Lord. You cannot hear it, but you see it in their eyes. You feel the coldness of it in the air that you breathe. We are afraid, Lord, that if we think non-analytical, imprecise, unsystematic, disorderly thoughts, they will shackle us further, until our hearts are unable to beat under the heavy chains. So we dare not use our minds.

We dare not eat with our naked fingertips, walk in generous groups, speak merrily in booming voices and laugh our mqombothi *laughs. They will scold us if we dare, not with their lips, Lord, because the laws prevent them from doing so, but with their eyes. They will shout, "Stop acting black!" "Stop acting black!" is what they will shout. And we will pause, perplexed, unsure of what that means, for are we not black, Father? No, not in the malls, Lord. We may not be black in restaurants, in suburbs and in schools. Oh, how it nauseates them if we even fantasise about being*

31

black, truly black. The old rules remain and the old sentiments are unchanged. We know, Lord, because those disapproving eyes scold us still; that crisp air of hatred and disgust crawls into our wide-open nostrils still.

Fikile tells us that our bill is ready, and that she will return in a 'sec' to collect our payment. Daddy is in the men's room so Mama smiles a nod at Fikile. Daddy will pay when he returns. The swinging door knocks against the back of my chair as Fikile re-enters the kitchen. She did that on purpose, I would say to Tshepo if he was here, but I slide my chair closer to the table and say nothing because Tshepo is not here. What's her problem? Nobody asked for the bill anyway, Tshepo might say in response.

When Old Virginia tired of trying to chase Tshepo away and gave in to the little boy who would follow her around the house with his toy broom, mop and dustpan set, she would empty her bucket, set down her multipurpose rag and lead Tshepo outside to the grass where she would seat him on her lap and tell him stories. When Tshepo grew too smart for Old Virginia and found it inappropriate to follow her around, he led me into the garden to tell me stories of the stories Old Virginia once told.

Let us remember that time of old.
...Nkano
We will all appreciate that things were a lot quieter then.
...Nkano

We will recall that we could hear then.
...Nkano
We remember the story of the Green Apples and Pears.
...Nkano
How great it was to be a Green Apple. How unfortunate to be a Pear.
...Nkano
"But are they all not fruit?" you ask.
...Nkano
Yes indeed.
...Nkano
But these, sadly, are the ways of our world.
...Nkano
We remember that then it was thought that there was no reason for them to grow on separate trees.
...Nkano
They were so similar and yet so different.
...Nkano
How beautiful it was to see one grow alongside another.
...Nkano
But the Green Apples grew bold,
...Nkano
while the Pears were unaware.
...Nkano
The Green Apples grew proud,
...Nkano
while the Pears were unaware.
Nkano
The Green Apples grew evil thoughts,
...Nkano
while the Pears were unaware.

33

...Nkano

It was only after much growing had been done that the Pears awoke.

...Nkano

Of course, we will all appreciate that by then it was too late.

...Nkano

We recall how many Pears were found smashed against the stony earth.

...Nkano

We recall their stems bent and broken.

...Nkano

We remember the deep bruising, the ruptured flesh, the oozing.

...Nkano

But worse, we remember those Pears that lay in the dirt and did not bruise or ooze at all.

...Nkano

We cried for those Pears,

...Nkano

we cried because we knew that those were the young, whose flesh had never reached ripening, but had been yanked off the tree all the same by the bold, proud and evil Green Apples.

...Nkano

"But are they all not fruit," you cry, "of the same tree?"

...Nkano

Yes indeed.

...Nkano

But these, sadly, are the ways of our world.

...Nkano

But do we recall?

...Nkano

The day a Pear tore off a Pear from the Green Apple and Pear tree and threw it against a rock?

...Nkano

We had been told that this Pear had developed differently, without the long neck that was common to Pears, and with a fuller and rounder lower body.

...Nkano

Of course, this was nothing new to us or to the Pears and perhaps to some of the Green Apples, for fruit often took on strange forms.

...Nkano

When the Pear tore off a Pear from the Green Apple and Pear tree and threw it against a rock, there grew a wild commotion in the tree.

...Nkano

The women wailed and the men swore to capture and kill the traitor Pear. For who had ever heard of such a thing? A fruit attacking one of its own?

...Nkano

We will appreciate that things were a lot quieter then.

...Nkano

And these things we could hear with our own ears.

...Nkano

The traitor Pear, sensing his life was in danger, ran before the king of the Green Apples and begged for his protection.

...Nkano

"I am a Green Apple, my King," the Pear pleaded.

...Nkano

"Do I possess the long neck that is common to those worthless Pears and their raindrop-shaped body? No, my King. I am a Green Apple, born from and raised by

35

a Green Apple. I only killed that Pear to help rid our tree of those parasitic Pears. Please, my King, grant me your protection."

...Nkano

And so a Pear became a Green Apple.

...Nkano

Ah, it is the workings of the world,

...Nkano

that things will grow.

...Nkano

And grow they did.

...Nkano

With time the traitor Pear grew the neck that was common to Pears.

...Nkano

But the traitor Pear was unaware.

...Nkano

With time the traitor Pear grew a raindrop-shaped lower body that was common to the Pears.

...Nkano

But the traitor Pear was unaware.

...Nkano

We remember the day,

...Nkano

because it was after that day that it was thought better that Pears and Green Apples should grow on separate trees.

...Nkano

We remember the day,

...Nkano

because the sky was clearer than it had ever been.

...Nkano

It was on this day that the traitor Pear decided, with

the sky being so clear and all, that he would go out and sun himself, before the world awoke and work had to be done.

...Nkano

What an unfortunate notion.

...Nkano

It was on this day, when the sky was clearer than it had ever been, that the Pear, sitting out in the sun, his neck grown long, his lower body raindrop-shaped, was thought to be a Pear.

...Nkano

And of course, it being so early, he had not yet had the chance to rub his skin against the leaves to make it shine like that of a Green Apple.

...Nkano

And of course he, being a Green Apple for so long, had forgotten to be careful.

...Nkano

Why, he was so close to the other Green Apples, having proved himself through numerous dead Pears, that he believed for sure that the Green Apples saw him as one of their own.

...Nkano

What an unfortunate notion.

...Nkano

The traitor Pear, sitting out in the sun, looking up at a clear sky, unaware of a few Green Apples drawing closer, his neck grown long, his lower body raindrop-shaped, was yanked off the tree and thrown against a rock.

...Nkano

Just like any other Pear.

...Nkano

This is where the story ends.

As Daddy hands our payment over to Fikile, who stands impatiently at the edge of our table, I wonder if anybody has ever told her this story.

Belinda's parents had a waterbed in their bedroom. It was a drab room with poor ventilation and an unusually low ceiling. The striped navy-blue and cream wallpaper was peeling off, revealing pretty pink tulips beneath, stuck there by a previous family. It seemed the sun, like Father Christmas and my house, preferred not to enter this house.

I hated being indoors at Belinda's. My clothing always managed to collect dog hair from everything I made sure I did not touch, and although I didn't mind it as much as I minded the smell, I knew Mama would shout at me for bringing 'that filth!' home again. The Johnsons lived on a large plot in Randjiesfontein. When the sun was outside the door and high, Belinda and I would roam the garden searching for four-leafed clovers that Belinda said would bring us good luck if we chewed them. When I told Mama about our clover-leaf lunch – which tasted of dog urine – she was horrified, that it was to be expected from these people to attempt to poison her only daughter, and after making me gargle with Anti-Germ, Mama threatened to prohibit me from visiting Belinda again if I ever accepted any kind of food from the Johnsons.

I knew that Mama was serious, but I actively partook in all the Johnson family feasts anyway. From asparagus quiche to cabbage sandwiches, I ate it all. I liked Belinda and her queer family even if they did have a peculiar palate. Mrs Conradie had seated Belinda and me together in grade three and we had been Best Friends Forever and Ever, ever since. On rainy days Belinda's mother would lay out newspapers and give us a scrap piece of canvas to colour with Belinda's finger-paints. We would lie on the floor of the Johnson's studio, swinging our legs in the air and painting mermaids and unicorns while Belinda's mother sat at her wooden table sketching stuffed birds.

I remember when Belinda's mother kicked us out of the studio for giving her a migraine. I did not ask Belinda what a migraine was, because Belinda liked to think she knew everything. Belinda's father was outside setting bird traps when we got on our knees and discreetly crawled into Belinda's parents' bedroom at the end of the narrow passage. The microscopic grey and white television was on the Oprah Winfrey show. I remember the guests on the show were teaching Oprah the Night Train Jive. Belinda and I rolled around the floor in stitches as Oprah and her guests formed a train and jiggled around the room going 'oh-ah' to the Night Train theme song. Jumping onto the waterbed, we too formed our own two-man train, going 'oh-ah' until Belinda's mother kicked us out of the house into the rain, laughing.

When I spot Belinda and her father coming out of The Bread Lady across from Silver Spoon, I change direction and enter the pharmacy on my right. I suppress the twinge of guilt that threatens to knot my stomach. Belinda will not be thrilled to see me either, I tell myself.

After-Sun. Bikini. Ballet. Barbie and Ken. Cruise. Disneyland. Disco. Diamonds and Pearls. Easter Egg.

Fettuccine. Frappé. Fork and Knife. Gymnastics. Horse Riding. Horticulture. House in the Hills. Indoor Cricket. Jungle Gym. Jacuzzi. Jumping Jacks and Flip Flacks. Khaki. Lock. Loiter. Looks like Trouble. Maid. Native. Nameless.

No, not me, Madam. Napoleon. Ocean. Overthrow. Occupy and Rule. Palace. Quantity. Quantify. Queen of England. Red. Sunscreen. Suntan. Sex on the Beach. Tinkerbell. Unicorn. Oopsy daisy. Unwrap them all at once! Video Games. World Wide Web. Wireless Connection. Xmas. Yoga. Yo-yo Diet. You, You and You. Zero guilt.

Tshepo reckons that it is inevitable that one's circle of friends will become smaller as one grows older. He reasons that when we begin we are similar, like two glasses of water sitting side by side on a clean tray. There is very little that differentiates us. We are simple beings whose interests do not extend beyond playing touch and kicking balls.

However, like the two glasses of water forgotten on a tray in the reading room, we start to collect bits. Bits of fluff, bits of a broken beetle wing, bits of bread, bits of pollen, bits of shed epithelial cells, bits of hair, bits of toilet paper, bits of airborne fungal organisms, bits of bits. All sorts of bits. No two combinations the same. Just like with the glasses of water, Environment, jealous of our fundamentality, bombards our basic minds with complexity. So we become frighteningly dissimilar, until there is very little that holds us together.

"Who are you, Ofilwe? You do not know who you are."

"Oh and I suppose you do. You have me all figured out. Right? You have all the answers. What is it that you want from me, Tshepo? What is it that you would like me to do? Burn their photos? Tear up their letters? Act as if I never knew them? Oh, and to make it really authentic, maybe I should pretend that I cannot swim, Tshepo. Like you do. What a marvellous idea! That, right there, would make me real: prove to you, dear brother, and the whole wide world that I know who I am."

"Are you not tired, Ofilwe?"

"I am tired of you, Tshepo."

"When will it be enough? When will you realise that they only invite you when Tamara and Candice cannot make it? When there is an extra seat? When will you realise that the parents permit it because their children find you cute?"

"Leave me alone, Tshepo. I have to get ready."

"So you are going to go tonight to this – what is it? Dinner? And naturally, being the cultivated sweetheart you are, politely listen to them talk about their music, their boyfriends and their holidays abroad? Oh and maybe, out of courtesy, they'll drop in a 'You're looking great, Fifi' before getting back to the agenda of who's hosting who at Crystal Bay this Christmas."

42

"Kristen Bay."

"Whatever, Ofilwe. What does it matter? Are you going to Kristen Bay this Christmas? Do you even know where these lovely bays are that you spend your evenings talking about? Do you not feel like a fool, taking part in conversations that have nothing to do with you? Conversations that will never have anything remotely to do with you. You are the backstage crew in the drama of their lives. If they need you, they do not know it and do not care. Open your eyes."

"Stop it, Tshepo. These are my friends you're talking about."

"Friends, Ofilwe, know your name. Friends ask where you come from and are curious about what language you and yours speak. Friends get to know your family, all of them, those with and those without. Friends do not scoff at your beliefs, friends appreciate your customs, friends accept you for who you really are."

"Get out of my room, Tshepo."

Their faithless eyes crawl on my skin, making it itch. I scratch my neck. Perhaps if I walk over to the topical creams section, they will ease off. The pharmacist himself is tolerable, decades have a way of redeeming one. It is his spinster of a sister I detest. I know it is only a matter of time until she slithers over to offer me her unasked-for assistance. Seeing Belinda has put me in sour spirits and I am in no mood to use the accent today. I hold my breath as I walk between the security sensors, and out of the pharmacy doors, daring them to ring wildly. Who knows, maybe I do have an innate proclivity for theft.

Samantha Grey's father wanted her back. She'd smugly spill it all as we sat in a circle on Mrs Mark's mat, 'sharing and caring' during Guidance. He wanted custody and would pay any price to win her and too-fast-for-even-the-fast-girls Lucy back from bi-polar Mom and her boyfriend of the week. It was rational to pity her, but as we watched item after recently bought item slip effortlessly off cherry-gloss lips, we envied her and bargained with the gods that they should be so gracious as to let divorce rain down on our poor households, too. Mrs Mark, eyes soggy and face swollen in dismay, suggested that we give Samantha a group drukkie. In our arms Samantha promised that if we proved to be as cool as her friends from her previous school she would consider asking her Dad if we could spend a weekend at the dam.

I had heard of the kissing game spin-the-bottle, and thought, already wise at only twelve, that it was cowardly to allow a deodorant can (apparently it pointed better than a bottle) to determine who and when you embraced. I knew that at the right time with the right guy I would embrace all I liked without seeking the approval of any type of container. That is why when we sat in a circle on Samantha's Dad's polished floor watching the Axe deodorant can spin recklessly, I thanked my guardian angel that there was no right guy here and this was not the right time.

*As the Axe was spun again, I knew from the way it
had been mocking me with its sarcastic swirls all night
that it would point at me next. It was too late to fake a
sunstroke-related headache, so I silently pleaded with it
to pair me up with a girl. Any girl. Anything rather than
the humiliation of exposing my inexperienced lips to the
expertise of those that belonged to the boys in the room.
The conniving canister instead commanded that Clinton
be the one I kiss. Clinton Mitchley. The Clinton Mitchley
who was believed to have taken his first girl at the age of
ten. Samantha's Clinton. My intestines choked. I knew
that the longer I sat staring at the abominable piece of
aluminium, the harder it would be to do the deed. I
calmly shifted my bum, still in wet board shorts, into
the centre of the circle. I gently helped myself onto my
knees, closed my eyes and pouted out.*

"No ways! Her lips are too dark!" he protested.

*Now with eyelids fastened tight (No ways! Her lips are
too dark), I shifted back to my ready spot (No ways!
Her lips are too dark), unsure of what to do next (No
ways! Her lips are too dark), whispering the words to
myself (No ways! Her lips are too dark), not believing
that they were spoken words (No ways! Her lips are
too dark); live words (No ways! Her lips are too dark);
words that had been followed by an explosion of
general laughter (No ways! Her lips are too dark).*

I curse the pharmacist's sister for making me leave
the shelter of her shelves of medicine. The pathway
I have chosen to take me to Mama, who I suspect is
in Supermart, is the same one Belinda and her father

are on and now they have seen me. I swear never to support that pharmacy again. The paved pathway is bordered by silver bars on either side. The bars are linked with cable. Long and narrow, these pathways encourage congeniality amongst the shoppers of Little Square but offer you no space to escape interaction with approaching strangers, forcing one of you to stop and step aside, smile a wooden hello, and let the other pass.

Dear Fifi:

How are you? I never see you anymore! What is going on? I miss you. Got so much to tell you! How come you never reply to my letters anymore? I've been sticking them under your desk like we always do. Have you not been getting them? (Maybe they've been falling off.) I mean it, I really do miss you. Are you cross with me over the whole late library book thing? I'll pay the fine, Fifi; it's really no biggy. I'm sorry, though, if that's the issue. Remember our promise, our No Secrets Policy? That was good or bad secrets, remember? No Secrets, good or bad. SO if there is anything wrong, you are obliged, by the sacred Best Friends Book of Rules and Regulations for the sake of all Best Friends, to come, to tell me. He he☺ I mean it.

Gosh. I really do miss you. I've said that a lot, haven't I? What is happening to us, Fi? I don't even know you anymore. Anyway, Mrs Swart is looking at me funny. I finally understand why you hate this woman. Gosh. Why is she even dressed like that in the first place? I should be looking at her funny. She should be looking in the mirror and looking at herself funny. Maybe she doesn't have a mirror. Who dresses like that in this day and age? Fifi, it is frightening. Fortunately for you, Fi, I cannot bring myself to defile this pretty piece of paper with a description of the ensemble she has on. How are we supposed to get an education with her prancing around the classroom like that? It is a lack of consideration, that is what it is. Pure selfishness. OK, now she is really looking at me funny so I should wrap this up. Well, I guess I kinda said all I really wanted to say. Hi and I miss you. Tried calling. You are never home these days, Old Virginia mentioned something about 'he busy being out'. Ha ha!☺ But you know good Ol' Virginia never could get anything right. I actually, at first, thought you were avoiding me, and then I came back to my senses: Best Friends for Life means best friends for life! (Right?)

Maybe we can do a sleepover this weekend. Like old times! You choose the movies. I swear to shut up this time. Last weekend at Renee's we had hot chocolate with a dash of Amarula and cream. It is to die for, Fi! We can try make some of that too. Gosh, it's been so long! I'm excited now. Please write back this time. You can't pretend you didn't get this one. I'll put it ON your desk. Will call you tonight. Answer the phone please! (Old Virginia makes no sense.) Promise to let you play with my hair for as long as you like if you come over. I swear.

Lots of Lekker Love

Belinda
B.F.F.E

47

I will greet Belinda and her father just as soon as they get closer. I could still pull off escaping into another store, but I won't because that would make them think I am ashamed, and I am not.

I told myself I was throwing out all the garbage in my life when I rejected their invitations. I told myself that this detox had been a long time coming, when I felt nothing when she began to cry. I told myself that now I would finally be happy when I took their pictures off my wall. I tried to say it day and night, hoped I'd chant it in my sleep, just until my foolish eyes stopped watering, the stubborn boulder in my throat dissolved and I began to believe that I was really 'better off' without them. Because I really am.

I feel sorry for Belinda. I feel sorry for me. But I guess that's just how the cookie crumbles. Things do not always work out the way they should. I think at heart she is a good person. But I am a good person too. She meant well. But we were different. And somewhere between grades three and ten that became a bad thing. It hurts hurting your friends. But she hurt me. You miss the laughs, the delirious things you'd do and the madness you shared.

But after a while it's agony playing a role you would never dream of auditioning for. You fall ill from explaining why Mama does not shave. You run out of excuses why Daddy refuses to go fishing with the rest of the dads, and why Koko won't help out at the tuckshop like everybody else's grandmother does. Even if Felicity, the only other girl of African descent in your grade, and the three other brown kids in the younger years, treat you like the scum they believe they are, at least you are all the same. At least they don't stare or question or misunderstand.

"Say 'uh-vin' Fifi. You bake a cake in an 'uh-vin', not 'oh-vin', 'uh-vin'."

"This is boring, Belinda, let's see who can climb the highest up that tree."

"No, Fifi! You have to learn how to speak properly."

"I can speak properly."

"No you can't, Fifi. Do you want to be laughed at again? Come now. Say 'uh-vin.'"

"Uuh-vin."

"Good. Now say 'b-ird.' Not 'b-erd', but 'b-ird'.

I am not used to hating. Hate sits heavy on my heart. It reeks. I can smell it rotting my insides and I taste it on my tongue.

Daddy hands over his bankcard to Mama so that she can draw out her money for the week. When Daddy decided, two or three years ago, that nursing was too demanding for his apparently overworked wife, who he believed would be better off spending her time at

No. 2064 Honeysuckle Street raising their potentially wayward children, they agreed that he would give her a weekly allowance to cover her daily expenses.

February can be scorching hot in Little Valley and today it's just that. Putting his arm around my shoulder, Daddy whispers, loud enough for Mama to hear, that I will be his eyes and make sure that our spendthrift mother does not draw out more cash than she is supposed to. Daddy winks. Mama smirks, and walks away. I do not wink back, but follow after Mama, mildly annoyed. The banking centre is on the other side of the parking lot. The heat is overwhelming and I am uncomfortable being alone with Mama.

Do all South Africans think in English? Is that a stupid question? Do you think if we were to do a Cross Sectional Study of Thought Analysis in a Population of South African People we would find that there is a language difference between our generation and the last? How does it work? Is that a stupid question too? Thought seems almost involuntary. I'm sure even the dimmest of minds engage in some form of thought, some kind of internal communication.

I don't think people consciously decide to engage in thought in the first place. There is probably a standard level of thought and under certain stimuli, like during end-of-year examinations and HIV tests, it spikes and brings itself to your attention. So then, how is it determined that I will think in English and Mama will think in Sepedi? Perhaps thought is as uninspiringly simple as an intrapersonal extension of the interpersonal communication we engage in, in our day to days.

"Oh!" Mama exclaims, as she raises her handbag to shield her face from the glaring sun that beats wickedly on our heads. "I am sure I am losing complexion as we speak."

I didn't feel bad. Mama didn't go to high school, so what was the point of telling her about the parents' evenings? In theory, parents' evenings are there to give parents an opportunity to assess their children's scholastic progress, to ascertain if all milestones are being achieved and determine where their dear little Bo ranks amongst the rest of his peers. In practise it is an exhibition night, where teachers cover their tables in floral prints and set them up outside their classroom doors. It is here in the corridors of learning where the teachers proudly showcase their works of erupting volcanoes, provincial debating league trophies and interschool 100m sprint medals. It is a night out at the gallery, where children, in their longest school skirts and most diligent shirts, display to each other their accomplished parents, linked at the elbow, necks wrapped in matching scarves, but especially to the teachers they commonly avoid. Mama would not understand any of that. I care about her, that is why I didn't want to put her through all of that. Besides, Mama's English is ghastly.

My Mama is beautiful. At forty-six she has skin as soft as the underside of a newborn's foot. Drops of black ink dot the centres of her eyes and wild, knotted eyelashes frame them. My Mama is a metallic blue-black in colour. My Mama is a giant. My Mama was not supposed to be, not with that foreign skin anyway, but my Mama is. Daddy sought controversy, marrying a metallic blue-black nothing girl of a nothing woman and a man we know only as 'Irrelevant'. Even amongst the poor there are those who are poor and even amongst the lower class there are those who are lower class. Perhaps it is consoling for us that there is always some who are worse off: they are a group who are dumped with the heap of scorn that has been offloaded onto our own heads.

But still, it would be lazy to accord all the credit to Daddy. Mama has her own might. It's a life of nothingness when you are a nothing girl with a metallic blue-black skin. But it is too easy to ration the rest of the credit to her. No, it belongs to the man who is Irrelevant. He was only spoken of once in my life. I remember the way the teacup fell from Koko's hand, the way she let it fall, when he was mentioned. "Irrelevant" is all she had said in response to my question. She had then stood lifeless for a million years, allowing the spilt black tea to dry up around and crawl under her swollen feet.

I figure Irrelevant had come from somewhere close to the equator. In my mind he is a warrior. He is a prophet. Or he is a teacher, moved by the story of a lost child in a forgetful world. On a journey in the South, he met a girl called Koko and they fell in love. But she refused to fight, to run, to believe or even to learn, and the rest became 'irrelevant'.

I walk slightly behind Mama so that I may examine her from a better angle. She spins all types of heads wherever she goes. Women look. Men stop and look. I bet they wonder how one with a metallic blue-black skin can walk so high. I want to hold her hand so that they may see that she is mine, confirm that her blood, Irrelevant's blood, runs through my veins and that some day perhaps I will look somewhat similar. But Mama and I do not hold hands. It is not something we do.

I am so embarrassed. I do not know if I will ever live this down. What if Karen and Lisa tell the other girls? Then nobody will ever sleep over at my house again. Can you believe Mama? She was so excited she ran up the stairs and phoned Koko to tell her that white people were coming over to spend the night at our house. The way she carried on. It was as if my friends were coming over to see her. She never left us alone, not once. Not even to breathe. She kept knocking on my door poking her nosy face in, asking us (in her broken English) if we needed anything. I wanted to die. I wanted her to die. The next morning Mama ran baths for the girls. Did she not know that white people only bathe at night? I am so embarrassed. Mama is dumb. I told her that after they had left.

Mama stands in the Persons Bank queue while I absent-mindedly flip through the magazines on the shelf outside the second-hand books and antique store. It occurs to me that perhaps it would have been appropriate to have offered to stand in the queue for Mama, something Tshepo would have done instinctively. The queue is long. The sun is hot. Why did she not ask me to?

It is because I am smart and speak perfect English. That is why people treat me differently. I knew from a very young age that Sepedi would not take me far. Not a chance! I observed my surroundings and noted that all those who were lawyers, doctors and accountants, all the movie stars that wore beautiful dresses, all the singers that drove fancy cars and all my friends who owned the latest clothing, did not speak the language that bounced berserkly from Koko to Tshepo to Malome Arthur to Mama and back to Koko again. I did not care if I could not catch it.

I spoke the TV language; the one Daddy spoke at work, the one Mama never could get right, the one that spoke of sweet success.

How can I possibly listen to those who try to convince me otherwise? What has Sepedi ever done for them? Look at those sorrowful cousins of mine who think a brick is a toy. Look at me. Even the old people know I am special. At family reunions they do not allow me to dish up for myself. "Hayi!" they shout. "Sit down, Ofilwe." They scold my cousins for being so thoughtless. "Get up and dish out for Ofilwe, Lebogang!" They smile at me and say. "You, our child, must save all your strength for your books." Do you see, I always tell my cousins, that they must not despair, as soon as my schooling is over, I will come back and teach them English and then they will be special too?

Katlego Matuna-George, dressed in a Vanguard Creation, sells the cover of this month's *Fresh Magazine*. Katlego, the former principal dancer of the renowned Von Holt School of Modern Dancing, has just recently taken on the role of Lethabo Dlamini, Marx Dlamini's estranged twin sister, who was tragically stolen at birth, in *Yesterday's Tomorrow*, South Africa's oldest black soapie. When asked to describe how she spends her minimal free time off the set, Katlego shares that she tries to have as many equestrian weekends with her husband Tom at their farm in the north as possible. It helps to ground her and allows her the latitude to reflect on her life.

Mama and I return to the car in a silence similar to the one that accompanied us to the Banking Centre. It has not always been like this. In my memory Mama and I used to speak a lot. I would tell her everything, except the things she did not need to know. Mama knew that I desired to be an astronaut one day, and have a house in the southern hemisphere and another in the northern hemisphere so that I could avoid the winter. Mama knew that my favourite colour was green but that I hated peas. Mama knew that I wanted to have four children whom I would name Cloud, Claude, Claudia and Claudette but did not want the trouble of a man in my houses.

One day, while we were smashing pink tennis balls against the tall green court wall, Mrs Kumalo, our Physical Education teacher, blew her red whistle once. We quickly got into line, boys on the right and girls on the left, from shortest to tallest. Three unidentical white men in serious suits came down the court steps with Mrs Kumalo. Mrs Kumalo explained that these men were from the school governing board and that they were there today to write down how many different types of boys and girls we had in our grade one B class.

The fattest one said that he would read a short list of languages and that if we knew that was the language we spoke the most at our homes, then we should raise our hands up as high as we could so that the tallest one could count them. Mrs Kumalo added that the languages would be read out in alphabetical order and that she would ask Mrs Hill to explain to us what alphabetical order was when we got back to our classroom.

I was listening carefully, so was the very first one to raise up my hand, nearly as high as the tallest one's shoulder, when the fattest one read 'English'. "Put down your hand, Ofilwe," said Mrs Kumalo. Mrs Kumalo was always ugly to me, even when I never even did nothing. But I knew that I had better not back-chat, so I put down my hand and wondered when the bell would ring so that we could go back to our classroom where Mrs Hill would hopefully pick me to tickle her back.

When the three white unidentical men in serious suits had been through all the languages, the one that had not said a word yet muttered to Mrs Kumalo that I had not raised my hand when they were reading through the Bantu languages.

*"What language do you speak at home, Ofilwe?"
asked Mrs Kumalo, sounding a little bit mean again.*
*"English, Mrs Kumalo," I responded, confused because
I had raised my hand when the fattest one had read
out 'English,' but Mrs Kumalo had told me to put my
hand down.*
*"No, Ofilwe, what language do you speak to your
mother and father?" insisted Mrs Kumalo.*
"English, Mrs Kumalo," I tried again.

*Mrs Kumalo sent me to go stand with my nose against
the tall green court wall. As I walked away from
the three white unidentical men in serious suits, Mrs
Kumalo and the rest of my grade one B class, my nose
getting itchy, thinking that now Mrs Hill would never
choose me to tickle her back, I heard the one who had
not said a word until he did, say, "Just tick her under
'Zulu', it's all the same."*

Where does an unused language go? Is it packed away
in an old crumbly cereal box along with a misplaced
tomato, your old locker code, first telephone number
and the location of your budgie's grave, and then
shoved into the dusty garage space of your brain? Or
is it blown up or deleted or is it shredded up into a
gazillion fragments or degenerated or decomposed into
a nasty smell and excreted out of your body? Could it
all possibly be flushed away? My own tongue escaped
from me completely? That cannot be. Mama and Daddy
speak it all the time, although not to me nor to each
other. But surely my eardrums filter in some of that?

Parmesan cheese, pineapple and a modest amount of peppadew in a light salad cream sauce lathered on two grilled chicken fillets. The night was flawless, and I had remembered not to eat the garnish. A cup of café mocha, by then baby-bath warm, had to be gulped down. It was evident that the Rent-a-Taxi driver was slightly vexed. Had we kept him waiting that long? Climbing into the green kombi, I glibly threw an apology into the air. I did not care if he had heard me or not. I was celebrating sixteen years of life. I had paid for everything and I was paying him. It was my day.

Perfection: the ribbon of yellow street-lights illuminating the charcoal Jozi sky, the deserted road ahead, my sweetheart's hand in mine, Zandi, Mpho, Siphokazi, Tammy, Xolani, Maggi and Zee singing along to an old Tevin Campbell song on the radio, everybody laughing, laughing for me, boyfriend and best friends there because of me. Me, happy to be me.

Siphokazi changed the topic of conversation. IsiZulu, isiXhosa, sePedi, seTswana. Tongues flared, now dancing to a different kind of music. She spoke of what she called home-home, not the urban house she lives in now, but the home-home they left behind in the rural Eastern Cape. He laughed at the memory of the stubborn red mud that he remembered too, and how he thought he was the only one who battled to get it off his shoes after half a day's walk. They all reminisced over mornings spent splashing in blue plastic buckets, squirming away from grannies who scrubbed them a little too hard. Maggi recollected a tiny room with a mud floor squashed full of cousins sleeping side by side, all dreaming of the same sunrise. Everyone recognised the importance of the passing of these words, as each girl and boy shared their clan names and the histories behind them.

'Tlou' is ours, Tshepo later said, and 'Sereto' the poetry behind it. I had repeated the words over and over again, desperate not to forget. How foolish I must have looked, sitting there silently with not a thing to share. How angry I was at Siphokazi for shattering my night and at Tshepo for always having an answer for everything and at myself.

I decided not so long ago to take it a word at a time. The plan was that in every spoken sentence I would try to use a single word of Sepedi. Just like an athlete, I would gradually increase the workload until eventually I would be strong and fluent.

"Ke mang yo, Tshepo?"

"This is my sister, Ofilwe."

"She looks like a 'I want my Mommy!'"

"Leave Vuyo and I alone, Ofilwe, and go play inside with the other girls."

"Since I've been here I've only heard this little girl speak English. Do you only speak English, sweetie?"

"Vuyo, please man, leave her alone, she's young.

Ofilwe, I said go and play inside with the other girls."

'How hard could it be?' I had asked myself. 'Of course I can speak the language,' I had told myself a numerous times, 'I just don't because I have no reason to.'

"Daddy, Tshepo's calling me names!"

"Just ignore him."

"He called me an Aunty Jemima, Daddy."

"What is an Aunty Jemima?"

"Tshepo says an Aunty Jemima is a sell-out. Daddy, Tshepo says I am a sell-out. He says I embarrass him and that I mustn't ever come near him when his friends are around."

"Just ignore him, Ofilwe."

The plan was to try out my new vocabulary on Daddy first. I knew his mind was always elsewhere, so was certain that if I sounded relatively normal, he would respond with the usual 'OK, Ofilwe' and 'Don't worry Ofilwe'. It was only when I'd finished scheming, plotting graphs and typing out my method, that I realised how many gaping holes I had in my head. There I was battling to put sentences together, speaking in the slightest of whimpers, hoping that Daddy would pretend, out of pity, that he understood so that I would not be forced to repeat the mumbo jumbo I had spewed out. Each word ended in a shudder, a cringe.

Sometimes I just wish I could hold my breath just for a little while, and then a little while longer, until I do not have to hold it anymore. I do not like looking at later, because I do not understand what I see. If I just held my breath, for a small long while, then I wouldn't have to be there, and that would be OK.

Do you think if I closed my eyes real tight and held them that way for a forever amount of time, that when I tried to open them again, they would refuse, because they'd gotten comfortable being that way? Because maybe then I wouldn't have to see, and then I wouldn't have to feel so sad. I do not like to watch what you do to yourself, little black girl. I do not like to see you sell your soul for a silver skin. Why do you pull at your button nose? Do you not see that it is beautiful that way? I do not know how to fix you, little black girl, so I will shut my eyes as tight as I can.

I hate my ears, for they are the greatest liars I have ever known. They lie to me every day. As soon as I speak a word they play it back to me in an accent that is not my own. Perhaps my ears are thieves too. "Whose accent is this?" I demand to know. They are not intimidated by my rage. "Whose accent did you steal, you lying thieves?"

Oh, sometimes I want to cut my toes, just one and then another, until I cannot cut them anymore. If I had no toes, it would be so difficult to walk. Then everybody would say, "Sit down, poor little black girl. Sit down, and do not wear yourself out so." Right there I would sit and not take another step. That would be OK, too: I do not know where I am going anyway.

We are now finally on our way back home. Mama uses facial wipes to prepare her skin for the Deep Velvet that she will apply to her eyelids. The Tender Plum that was modestly brushed onto the apples of her cheeks this morning will not match the Indigo chiffon skirt she must change into as soon as we get home. It is the second Sunday of the month, time again for Mama, mama Julia, mama Caroline and mama Peggy to meet. These three ladies are Mama's closest friends from a larger group of thirteen women. In another era, in a different land with a less controversial history, none of these thirteen women would be friends because no two of them have anything in common. Except, of course, the one thing that they do have in common, the thing that is significant enough to be sufficient reason to keep thirteen conflicting characters as the best of buddies. All of these women are trying to forget.

I move closer to the window so that I can see Mama's reflection in the side mirror. I wonder if she can see me watching her and what she thinks of it if she can. She pulls the visor down and dabs a little bit of Zambuck on her eyebrows, tinted slightly lighter to match the colour of her beaded cornrows, then arches them up high. Our eyes cross as Mama looks down to search for another one of her Essential Handbag Cosmetics in her glittery sequin clutch purse; I immediately pull away and stare out of the window, creasing my forehead tight so as to appear as if I am deep in thought.

The Benedicts have a 'We start together and end together' policy. Well not policy, because that makes it sound too much like a rule, but rather tradition. It's hilarious because there are six of them in the family, a mother and father, three daughters and little Jimmy, the only boy, and each morning, before they officially awake, all four kids sluggishly head for the parents' bedroom to what they call the Start/Finish bed for the daily Benedicts Family Team Huddle. It's a scramble to see who can get into the bed first and secure themselves the warmest spot, even if it means stepping on mom's head or jabbing dad in the stomach in the process. The show always begins with somebody falling out of the bed and ends with mom hysterically dragging everybody, sometimes even dad, out of the room! Of course that kind of stuff only happens on TV. In real life people have to go to work.

I call this symphony 'Unfinished' because that is the only word I remember being able to pronounce when I read the title on the back of the CD cover. Tshepo once danced to this piece at one of his ballet concerts at the clubhouse. This is the only CD Daddy has ever bought and the one that perpetually howls in his car when he is not listening to the news. I find this kind of music invasive and not a taste I think I would like to acquire, as Daddy describes it. I wonder if it is really a taste in classical music that Daddy acquired or rather a taste of money that has led to his desire for all things that insinuate wealth and stability.

Mama does not like to be touched. I personally have never seen it happen but she tells me that her skin is sensitive and breaks out in rashes if it is in contact with human flesh for a prolonged period of time. Children's hands are especially lethal and cause her a ghastly amount of discomfort when and after she comes into contact with them. Mama suspects it is because children by nature are filthy and thus exacerbate her fussy skin's response to touch.

Mama appears to be content with her creation. She puts her sunglasses on and sits back in the seat. I am impressed. With a few handbag essentials and the help of the vehicle side mirror and front-seat visor, Mama has within minutes transformed herself from unassuming proud mother of two and grateful housewife to cosmopolitan woman-on-the-move. She will be in the house only long enough to swiftly change out of her pure white Sunday dress. Then she will be on the road again, off to swap scandals with the ladies over crushed ice and olives.

I wish I could have danced for Mama, but Lady Gertrude would not have me in her class. I was all angles: elbows and knees prodding out of every corner of my pre-pubescent square-shaped body. I should have been Tshepo and Tshepo me. Mama's Tshepi. I don't know if Tshepo ever really enjoyed the Pliés and Pas de Chats, or the baby-blue leotard and white lace on the satin slippers. I suppose it made no difference whether he did or not.

Tshepo was magnificent. His slight frame, sustained arms and legs, deft chin, precise nose, easy shoulders and delicate manner in which he swirled all across the portable stage and behind the curtains had the audience of doting mothers, envious sisters and well-meaning neighbours mesmerised. Tshepo had

65

everything that made Mama beautiful and the one thing that would have made her perfect: Daddy's fair skin. Tshepo always knew how to make Mama gleeful.

I had thought back then that if I could give my nose a name, then it would be easier to combat. At the end of grade five we went on a three-day school camp to Pilanesberg. On our first night we played a game called Mud Wars. I remember it was Bush Babies against The Dolphins. I was one of The Dolphins, but do not remember having anything to do with the inappropriate name of the group. We had been told to pack old clothing prior to our departure, and that is what we were wearing when our camp leaders collected us from our dormitories to direct us to the lake where the game would be held. Each team member was instructed to fetch a long stick from a pile that had been previously assembled by the camp leaders. The sticks were swirled in the gooey mud that formed the lake's boundaries, until a ball of wet sand, held together by pieces of grass, slime and insect remains, formed on the end. The objective was to hit as many of the opposition with mud balls as possible until all their men were down before ours were. I remember swinging my stick, aiming for a Bush Baby I had spotted hiding behind a heap of broken branches, and hitting the wall behind them instead. The mud ball hit the wall and stuck right there. While I stood there waiting for it to slide down, thinking that it looked a lot like my nose fixed stubbornly against the camp wall, I was hit by a Bush Baby in the back. So that is what I named my nose: Mud War.

"I bumped into Belinda Johnson outside the pharmacy," I say, stealing the spotlight from Symphony No. 8's piano piece, provoking one of them to respond.

"That's lovely, dear, we have not seen Belinda in a long while. Did you invite her over for lunch?"

"No, Daddy." That is a nonsensical question. Daddy knows very well that there will be no Sunday lunch today because Mama will be elsewhere. And I cannot cook, Tshepo will not cook and Old Virginia is not allowed to cook. Besides, is today not golf day, like every other day of the week?

"I have told you before, Daddy, Belinda and I are no longer friends." It is important that I focus on my objective and not allow Daddy's play-play world to annoy me.

"Those are good news, Ofilwe," Mama speaks at last.

"Good news? That is a terrible thing, Ofilwe."

"It is about time, my darling girl. Did not I say those people she were no good for you, Ofilwe?" Mama makes as if she cannot hear Daddy.

"It is careless to throw away a useful relationship such as yours and Belinda's, Ofilwe, without even giving it any thought. Those Johnsons are fine people."

"Fine people? If I is not forbidden you from accepting

food from those so-called fine people, Ofilwe, you would be dead now, wouldn't you, Ofilwe? I am sure, my girl, you are old now and now you can see yourself and be glad me, your Mama, she protected you from that rubbish that goes on at that farm, nê Ofilwe?"

"Those people are mighty intelligent, Ofilwe. You see white people, my child, they know how to utilise their money. Mr Johnson knows that it is wise to invest in property. Why do you think they live on such a large piece of land?"

"Sies! And that dirty house of theirs is a disgust. Remember, Ofilwe? Do you remember how dirty you is when you came back home, Ofilwe? No wonder you is always sick. Those people, they is made you sick, my child."

"Were you ever sick, Ofilwe? Nonsense! Those Johnsons are open-minded people, Ofilwe. Those are the kind of white people we need in our country. They treated you well, did they not, Ofilwe? How often was Belinda here to help you with your school work, Ofilwe?"

"That Belinda is fat and ugly, my child, and he is only your friend because nobody wants her. Her own people don't want him and now she wants to come to you? Hayi!"

"As soon as we get home you must call Belinda, Ofilwe, and sort out your differences. She is a reasonable young lady, I am certain she will be willing to put all of this behind her."

"Ofilwe, you just leave this thing alone. If she wants you come back, she must be the one who is making amends, and it will be no loss to you if he does not. You hear me, my girl? No loss. You must now be starting to be can surrounding yourself with the right kind of people, Ofilwe. Like that Melissa du Toit, Ofilwe, where is he now? What a charming girl."

I do not enjoy the bickering, but it is the only way to get Mama and Daddy to speak. The drive home seems longer than normal today and the wail of Daddy's music is anguish, this is my only deliverance. It may not sound like they are speaking to each other, but they are. I am like a telephone operator. I connect them, except instead of using a dialling tone I instigate an argument to do so. The 'Belinda and I are no longer friends' line always works well, because they both feel extremely muscular about it, and because it is not directly related to either of their own lives. It keeps things from being personal and hurtful. These conversations they think they are having with me are really arguments that they are having between themselves. Aside from them, Mama and Daddy do not speak very much at all. It is good to speak right?

So I reckon I am doing them a favour by inciting quarrels. I suppose I benefit, too. Sitting here silently at the back, listening to them ask me questions they answer for me, I use their debates to collect words for my Sepedi vocabulary list. Although their arguments follow the same pattern each time they have them, sometimes they use a word they did not use the last time, a word I mouth repeatedly so as to master the pronunciation. I fix the words in my brain so that they can be added to my vocabulary list when I get home. I figure, if all else fails, if I achieve nothing else, at least someday I will be able to argue in Sepedi.

Residents of Little Valley Country Estate use a hand sensor to enter through the booms at the main gatehouse. Guests use a separate entrance. Guests are only allowed in after their visit has been telephonically verified by the guards, with those whom they are there to see. Daddy greets the security guard who is writing down the number plates of the vehicles lined up at the Visitors to the Estate Admissions Gate with his left hand while his right hand commands the striped red-and-white poles to rise.

When Daddy's company, IT Instantly, won the Post Office tender in which Daddy had invested numerous golf balls, a thousand glasses of JC, endless swipes on the Diner's Club card and a professionally gift-wrapped ten diamonds and steel limited-edition Mitchell bracelet in, Koko advised that a thanksgiving ceremony would be fitting. That was the same year Mama cashed in her nursing retirement package and suggested we celebrate Christmas Day in Disneyland, Florida.

The day of the thanksgiving ceremony is the last memory I have of Daddy's family, the Tlous, and Mama's family, the Ledwabas, all being in the same space at the same time. Grandmother Tlou, her partner Pat and Aunty Sophia arrived first in Grandmother Tlou's 380SE gold Mercedes-Benz. Koko had spent the night at our house helping Mama and Tshepo prepare the traditional beer that Koko reminded Daddy needed to be offered, together with the blood of an animal and motsoko, to our ancestors as a token of our appreciation for the good fortune that had fallen on our family. The rest of the Ledwabas arrived in

71

dribs and drabs, some of them having to change taxis thrice to get to the cumbersomely located Little Valley Country Estate.

Despite Koko's counsel that it was wiser to organise the cow a day before the ceremony at the very latest, Daddy was still out, apparently having difficulty finding a suitable cow, when the last of the Ledwabas arrived. Mama's older brother, Malome Arthur, and his son Benjamin, sensing the tension in the house, laid out a towel on the lawn and explored the copious amount of alcohol Daddy had bought the day before. Ous Desire, Malome Arthur's girlfriend, and cousin Dukie quickly busied themselves with pots and spices in the kitchen, escaping the interrogation that Malome Arthur's daughters from a previous marriage, Kagiso and Portia, were being subjected to by Grandmother Tlou and Aunty Sophia over Romany Creams and Rooibos tea.

It was already 4pm when Daddy arrived with Bra Alex and Uncle Max, Daddy's business partners, and a young white man, probably no older than twenty, whom I had never seen before. At the end of the driveway stood a bakkie that held a subdued chicken in an unnecessary cage. Daddy carried in his hand a large blue refuse bag that dripped blood into the house and onto Mama's peach Persian carpet, making her scream. Daddy's eyes were wide and red, suggesting that he had been drinking, and Uncle Max had unbuttoned his shirt, allowing his large belly to protrude out unapologetically.

Daddy, detecting the growing unease in the room, explained that he was unable to locate a live cow that

72

was purchasable, and had instead opted to buy a chicken from the young white man who had been so kind as to offer to drop it off at the house. Daddy went on to say that he did, however, remember that Koko had stressed the importance of a cow, so Bra Alex had suggested that they buy a slaughtered one at the butcher and had requested that its blood be collected in a Tupperware dish so that it could be used for the ceremony.

Koko and Mama were silently washing the dishes when the Little Valley Country Estate security guards drove up our driveway in their Jeep vans. Daddy, Bra Alex and Uncle Max had left shortly after Malome Arthur slit the disturbingly willing chicken's neck open, allowed its blood to seep into the soil and mumbled a brief prayer that nobody heard. Tshepo was thus the one who received the letter of warning from the two security guards that explained that the couple in No. 2042 behind us had alerted them that we were sacrificing animals after they spotted a chicken hung up on our washing line. The letter warned that we were liable to be heavily fined because we had breached rules no. 12.3 and 15.1 in the Little Valley Country Estate Code of Conduct Handbook.

12.3 Residents of Little Valley Country Estate may not keep any wild animals, livestock, poultry, reptiles or aviaries or any other animals of the sort on the Estate grounds.

15.1 Residents of Little Valley Country Estate must avoid installing visible laundry lines, Wendy houses, tool sheds, pet accommodation and the like in areas that are visible from public view and must ensure that the above are screened from neighbouring properties.

Kicking aside the traditional beer that lay forgotten in a bucket on the floor collecting flying peanuts and bits of carpet, Grandmother Tlou and Pat excused themselves, saying that they had other engagements to get to. Aunty Sophia, as usual, followed them out. Once they had left, Mama dropped the household cleaner and goldilocks she had been futilely using to try to remove the blotches of a now-brown colour from her carpet and turned to Koko:

"You happy now, ma? Now that you was embarrassing me in front of the eyes of my in-laws and my neighbours. Now that you cover my carpet with blood, fill my kitchen with dirty flies and chased my husband away from her home. You had to make your presence be felt, nê ma? Everybody must know Koko is here. You could not just let a good thing be. No ma, you must insist that this witchcraft be performed. You must be reminding all of us of our backward ways. Did Arthur's drunked prayer of thanks please the gods, ma? Is the gods now happy? Or now must we perform another ceremony to find that out?"

Little Valley Country Estate sells itself as 'your rustic escape from the rat race.' Daddy says that there were many such developments coming up in the city when he bought our house because South Africans were attracted to the idea of a residential area right in the melting pot of the country but even more so to ones that also assured the 24-hour a day maximum security mandatory for survival in Johannesburg. Daddy, however, said that he fell for Little Valley because they had created the most captivating horse-riding trails within their estate, and although he did not ride, he said that they were reason enough to learn to.

Driving into the estate (strictly adhering to the 40 kph rule), we pass homes where little children forget to close their front doors when they run in, where teenage girls smoke cigarettes out of their bedroom windows so their parents may not know and leave them wide enough open for eyes taking walks in the streets to stroll in. I look into these Seventh Heaven-like homes, I smell their food and catch a glimpse of the portraits on their walls as we drive by. Now back home, outside our orange brick villa, I peer into our own windows and wonder what others see.

"Tuscan is the architectural style," the sales agent had said to Daddy. "A gem!" she had shrieked, "a house incomparable to any other." However, inside my home it is not the smell of sautéed prawns and ricotta stuffed pasta with mushroom sauce that wafts into the garden, but rather the sharp smell of *mala le mogodu*.

I do not know where I may have lived before, or who I may have been. I do know that this world is strange, though, and I somewhat of an anachronism. Locked in. Uncertain whether I have come to love this cage too. Afraid of the freedom that those before the time before-before knew. There is jeopardy in the sky.

Mama shouts Tshepo's name as she enters the house and heads up the salmon-coloured hefty stone spiral staircase to the bedrooms on the third floor. "Tshepo, come down and help your sister carry in groceries." The midday sunlight beaming through the punch skylights high above the staircase and the shy wisp of Mama's white dress as she hurries up the stairs remind me of a make-believe fairytale. In the tale a beautiful but damned princess runs up a twisted tower in a forgotten castle escaping the crafty dragon that has kept her hostage in a moonless dungeon below. She runs up to a radiant prince above who will slay the dragon and free her from a life of darkness.

I am already holding three large packets in each hand, but grasp onto the seventh with my left ring finger and pinkie. They are heavy, but the garage opens into the kids' pantry, which leads to the kitchen. I do not have far to go. If I speed-walk I should be able to get them all there without dropping and breaking anything.

"It's fine, Mama, I can manage on my own," I say more to myself than to anyone else whilst dropping the packets onto the oyster-and-pearl marble kitchen surface. I flinch at the force with which the two meet, realising too late that there are glass containers in some of the packets.

"Tshepo! Tshepo wee!" Of course Tshepo can hear Mama. Although the walls of our house are thickly plastered to give it a colossal appearance, and the ceilings beamed and soaring to make it look grand, the living space is intimate and the family bedrooms all open up onto the circular stone staircase, so that every sound formed on the third floor is equally shared in 360° before dissolving into the nothingness and fleeing through the skylights. "Tshepo! Tshepo sweetie, we is home." Tshepo is choosing not to hear her. Mama is choosing not to know.

In this house it is the parents who slam doors. It is the cherry-wood cupboard doors in Mama's all-mirrors dressing room that now swing open and slam shut. Mama is in a rush, she will rapidly remove her dress and cream pumps and change into the skirt and wrap top that will match the cork heels she has been searching for a reason to wear. "Tshepo! Tshepo my darly. Tshepo!" I can still hear Mama from two floors down. She seems to delight in calling his name, despite the fact that she knows he will not answer. Persisting consoles her. "I never did stop trying," she will say to her friends when he is gone for good. "Never did I ever give up on him," she will continue, between sobs, as they rub her back in manicured sympathy.

I consider packing away the groceries but decide against it. What will I do with the mango atchar that steadily seeps through its cracks and collects at the bottom of the packet, turning the white plastic and the already soggy egg carton a grimy orange? Should I throw the whole plastic packet away? Is that not a waste of food? I do not even know where they keep the kitchen dustbin. Mama is always rearranging her kitchen. And where would I pack away the rest of the food? I am not sure what goes into the Kids' Pantry, Entertainment Pantry and Foods Pantry because it is all food to me. I will wait for Old Virginia to do it. Old Virginia should be around here somewhere.

"Tshepo, honey! Tshepo!"

I follow the mosaic of bundles of wheat on the soft-caramel tiled floor to my favourite room in the house. From here, right in the centre of the house you have a view of every nook that matters: the billiard room and its bar, the fishpond built deep into the floor of the sitting room, the lone fish that swims in its inky water, Daddy's newspaper room, the flat screen, the glass bricks that open out onto the outdoors and the breakfast table. From this room I can see it all. Other than when Mama is in here with her guests, this room is seldom used.

"Tshepo! Tshepo wee? Tshepo where are you?"

Through the window I see Daddy in the garden. It is a deliberate garden, meticulously arranged into several mazes of cleanly trimmed hedges bordering rugs of intense red and pink flowers which flatter the terracotta-tiled roof when they are in bloom. Standing in the heart of it in his Sunday suit, where all the mazes lead and where a clay boy wees into a stream of stones and pebbles below, Daddy resembles a character in a world of pretend. Although I cannot see from where I am sitting, I know my father is on his cellular telephone. I have known him for too long to kid myself into believing he is enjoying a moment of respite amongst the birds and shrubbery. Oh, but how picturesque it looks, Daddy, at home in the garden, framed by the window's silk curtains that are draped like ball gowns over the wrought-iron rods.

"Tshepo! Old Virginia, have you seen Tshepo? Tshepo! Where is my boy?"

It was something that was understood. Like the fact that Mama wakes up at 4.30am every morning. She wakes to intermittently stir the samp and beans which she had left in a pot to soak overnight so that they are soft and pulpy, ready for Daddy's breakfast at 7am (nothing else fills his stomach quite the same). It was something that was undisputed. Like the fact that Mama's money is her own to be used on herself and nothing else because she is beautiful and it costs money to remain so. It was something that was never questioned. Like the fact that Daddy has his lady friends, like Mama has hers too. And that Daddy sees his lady friends, like Mama sees hers too. So when Daddy scrambled down the stairs to the family room where Mama, Tshepo and I were watching the evening news, to point out that Tshepo had made an error in his university application forms (which Tshepo left on Daddy's study desk for him to sign), we all agreed that Tshepo had made an error indeed. In the space provided for 'Choice of degree or diploma' Tshepo had written 'Bachelor of Arts Majoring in African Literature and Languages' and not Actuarial Science, which Daddy and he had agreed upon.

Tshepo, contrary to his character, had begun the stampede of words. "I want to write," he stood up and declared, demolishing the shared notion that he had

79

made a mistake, "I want to speak. I want to say those things that people are afraid to hear. Those things that they do not want to face. In the pages of a book, in the privacy of their minds, where they feel a little less vulnerable, I will talk to them, long after the book is down, we will converse, my readers and I, and they will know."

"Nonsense!" Daddy bellowed. "Absolute nonsense."

"Stop it, John! Stop it." Mama's eyes were glistening. Clearly she had been moved by Tshepo's display.

"You are a lazy little bugger, Tshepo. That is what you are, bloody lazy."

"Leave the boy, John."

"You ran when you saw a challenge ahead. You didn't even have the guts to say it to my face. You disgrace me, Tshepo. You are a disgrace to our name."

"They is young, John. Let them dream."

"Dream, Gemina? Dream? Dream at whose expense? And then when he's finished dreaming, who supports the dreamer? You?"

"John, please. Stop all this. Tshepo, she is gifted. You know that. He is got talent and he is success in anything he is doing."

"Do not give me that rubbish, Gemina. You understand

nothing of the real world. You could not even finish high school."

And that is how it begun. After that comment, Mama shrieked and screamed so many sentences. Daddy roared a thousand others. Tshepo slipped between the panels of wood on the floor and disappeared. I sat there mesmerised. It was the longest conversation Mama and Daddy had ever had and it went on for days. When you thought it was sadly drawing to an end, it would abruptly begin again. At night the words they threw at each other would spin hysterically around, then fly through the innocent and exposed walls and into my room making me wake with delight. The words would swish up and come crashing down. They would zoom out of the door and back in again. They would dance on the balcony, and race down the stairs and spin in each other's arms.

I though it was fantastic. I had not seen Mama and Daddy so verbal with each other since before I can remember. "They're not talking, Ofilwe, they are fighting," Tshepo snapped at me after I had thanked him. What did it matter, didn't he see? Hadn't he heard? Mama and Daddy had been up the whole night, talking and talking and talking. "I couldn't even sleep, Tshepo! I tried, but I could not sleep," I laughed. Walking around the house in a warm and pleasurable drowsiness, hoping that it would never fade away, I quietly thanked my brother again for being so selfless.

"Where were you, Tshepo?" I ask. Tshepo turns around startled. He must have assumed I had left with Mama or Daddy. Tshepo holds a drum in his hands and is wearing a brightly coloured loose-fitting tunic, with wide elbow-length sleeves and a square neck. It resembles the West African shirts they sell at the flea markets.

"Where were you, Tshepo, did you not hear Mama calling you?" At first Tshepo looks a little embarrassed, but I think he decides against it, because he pulls the drum closer to his body, pushes his chest out and walks towards where he thinks I am sitting. He cannot see me.

"Where were you, Tshepo?" I ask again.

"In the middle." Ever since Tshepo started hiding out on the second floor, he decided that referring to the levels of our house as floors sounded pompous and that he would call the second floor the middle, the first ground, and the third the top.

"Did you hear Mama calling you?" I know he did and dared him to lie.

"No."

"You didn't hear her? She must have called you a gazillion times. You didn't hear that? She called your name from the moment she walked into the house, all the way up the stairs, while she was changing, all the way down again and on her way out. You never heard that, Tshepo?"

"No."

It is not the first time Tshepo has feigned absenteeism. In fact he does it all the time. It is something that developed discreetly. First he lacked an opinion about anything and then months later he ceased speaking altogether. Tshepo then became extremely busy with all sorts of projects and assignments. This was followed by a note, slipped under my bedroom door, that said he needed space to think and could no longer write in the newspaper room where the two of us had done our schoolwork from ever since we had work to do. Why, Tshepo was so very busy, he stopped having to come downstairs, then stopped having to go out, and then stopped having to be around until it was OK that Tshepo had stopped being. I taunt him not because I am sad for Daddy or sorry for Mama, but because sometimes I feel like Tshepo got the easy way out.

"What were you doing in the middle, Tshepo?"

"I was writing."

Tshepo, tracing my voice to the rocking chair, walks around the decorative coffee table, thoughtfully places the drum on the floor and sits down, cross-legged, on the sofa across from me. It is only now that I recognise his shirt as one of Mama's kaftans, presumably the white one that she once mentioned was too large. He must have dyed it.

"What are you writing?" Now that I have his attention, I resolve to say nothing about the kaftan which looks increasingly feminine and odd in the clashing blue, yellow and orange fabric paints he must have used. I wonder if they will wash out.

"A poem." And he begins to read.

We were the Sun's last hope: We whose skin had been marked by her fiery kiss.

We were all she had left to love and she promised to love us always.

Her rays turned pale skin a painful red. Her scorch crisped freckled noses and beat down on bleached heads.

Not out of vengeance. No, nothing they could ever do would bring her that low. Nor out of malice. Such hatred she had never known.

It was fear. Not fear of what she'd seen them do or what she'd heard them say. It was not fear of their extravagant rifles and armies of rigid men.

No, it was the hollow in their eyes and the cracks in their ice-cube hearts that scared her. She was afraid of the cold that threatened to seep out of their nothingness and smother her flame.

It was out of self-defence, Your Honour, that is why she burnt them. She had only seeked to protect herself and her own.

We were the Sun's last hope: We whose skin had been marked by her fiery kiss.

We were all she had left to love and she promised to protect us always.

But when it seems that all skin is pale, all noses freckled and all heads bleached?

It is not out of vengeance. No, nothing we could do would ever bring her that low. Nor out of malice. Such hatred she has never known.

No, it is the hollowing out of my eyes and the freezing over of your bubbling heart that scares her. She is afraid of the cold that threatens to seep out of our nothingness and smother her flame.

It is out of confusion, Your Honour, that is why she burns us. She only seeks to protect herself and find her own.

"Today I got new school shoes. Every year I scratch my new school shoes because I am clumsy and I trip and fall. But this year I am going to try my very best not to scratch my new school shoes. I am going to walk real careful and lift my new school shoes up high in the sky. This year I do not think I will scratch my new school shoes because I am now steady.

Mr Homes is my new teacher. He is a grade four

teacher and I am a grade four boy. It is funny, hey; all
the teachers in my school wear the same clothes, every
day. And I don't even know why, they just wear them.
They never even change. Maybe it is because they are
trying to make us feel better about having to wear
school uniform and stuff or maybe they just like their
clothes very much.

Mrs Leeroy's husband is a policeman. He has a funny
uniform. Sometimes he even comes to our school with
a gun. A real gun! He keeps it in his pocket, and Rick
says he heard Mrs Leeroy tell one of the grade four
teachers that he even sleeps with it at night! No way!
Rick is a liar! What if it goes off and shoots the roof?
Mr Leeroy would never do that.

Rick is so naughty, hey; just because his mom is a grade
seven teacher he thinks he can do anything he likes.
And he's a liar. One time I was cutting up my eraser
to give it to my friend who forgot his at home and
then I was going to give it to him, but I sort of forgot
and left it on Rick's desk and then Rick goes and tells
Mr Homes that I cut his eraser in half. And then Mr
Homes believes him and says, 'Tshepo I am giving you
a demerit for taking other children's property!' But I
knew I didn't take other children's property so I didn't
care. That's why nobody invites Rick to their parties
because he is a Meany.

I have a party to go to on the third. It is my second
indoor soccer party. Chad had one in grade three at the
clubhouse and now it is Tony's. If I feel like it I'm going
to be a professional soccer player one day, because I

86

am pretty good, but only if I change my mind about being a lawyer. Or maybe I'll be a computer man like Daddy, but I'll see. Mama says I can be anything I like in the whole world, even everything. But I don't think I want to be everything because then other people won't have jobs and stuff and then I'll feel real bad for them and then I'll have to give them all my money so that they can buy some bread and apples and juice and stuff and then I'll have no money and then I'll be poor.

At lunch break the other day we were playing horses and we were show-jumping over this one pole that used to belong to the jungle gym and then Craig was galloping backwards and then he tripped on Jason Shirley's juice bottle and then he fell and broke his whole wrist. But then he never even knew until he got home and his mom told him. They took him to an ambulance and then they put his wrist back together and then covered it with this real hard white stuff and when he came to school the next day he had to wear a different shirt because his big wrist wouldn't fit through his normal shirt. And then Jason Davey asked him if he could draw a picture on his wrist and then we just all ended up drawing, and Ben drew this funny picture of a girl that didn't even look like a girl, but looked like a house, and everybody laughed at Ben because Ben is so doff!

I kind of feel sorry for Ben though, because they live real far and he has to wake up extra early to get to school and stuff, but I guess it's his fault because there are a million schools in the world and he went and chose the furthest one. I'm lucky because I live in Lil' Valley Country Estate so if I feel like it I can even ride my bike to school. Maybe I'll ask for a new bike for my birthday and if I get one I won't scratch it and stuff because it will be all new and I won't even fall as much because I am now steady."

I was riding high on pink and purple plastic horses, going up and down and up and down and round and round and round and round on the merry-go-round of dreams and children's desires.

"Hello, my name is Ofilwe Tlou and I am eight years old. I have a Mama and a Daddy and a big brother and an Old Virginia and we all live in a house in Little Valley Country Estate. My Daddy makes computers and stuff and my Mama is a nurse and makes sick people better at this one hospital. My brother's name is Tshepo and he goes to another school for only boys. I don't go to his school because I'm not allowed to because they don't want girls there. When I told my brother that it hurts my feelings that his school doesn't like me and I never even did anything ugly, he said that I shouldn't be sad and that he'd tell his teacher that their rules are dumb and that maybe they'll change the rules after he tells his teacher but that even if they don't change their rules, he'll still be my friend anyway.

My brother is my favouritest friend because he's nice to me and he makes me laugh and stuff and he saves me all the red wine-gums and he plays with me everyday and he helps me with my homework and stuff and he chases away all the baddies out of my room at night and he tells me all his stories, even the secret ones and he reads me all his funny books and all sorts of other stuff. Oh, and I have a budgie called Yellow. That's all."

I just sit here. In this empty room. In an empty house. My head is full. My heart burst a long time ago. When I watch, when I listen, when I read, I must hold back. I cannot fall too deeply, believe too strongly or hold on too tightly to anything. Because how can I trust you – you mother, you father, you preacher, you teacher, you friend – when everything around me is a lie and all mercilessly trick me. I hate this cynicism that seeps through my veins. My mind is tired of reading through that barbed wire.

Except for Old Virginia's humming that comes from the laundry room outside, the world is silent. It is as if they are waiting for a response. A response from whom? I do not know. I have nothing to say.

No toddlers with snotty noses and grubby hands play in the streets in Little Valley Country Estate. Groups of teenage girls in bright T-shirts, old torn jeans and peak caps do not sit on the front lawn pointing and gossiping about the guys that walk past the gates of their homes. Older sisters do not play the *wailese* loud, so that those who know the tune can sing along as each mops, dusts and sweeps their homes clean. In Little Valley Country Estate the neighbours are the cars you see parked in their driveways and the children are the tennis balls that fly over the wall and into your pool.

Here at home, Tshepo was my only company and I his. Our motto was "Only Boring People Get Bored" and we swore to live each day by it. So as to prove that we were true to our word and that we were in no way boring people, each non-school day was a great adventure. We would make our own overalls by painting Daddy's large vests blue with the fabric paints that the previous owner left behind. We would collect knives, forks, sticks, screwdrivers and other such objects that resembled tools and go out and assist the builders where new houses were being developed. We would make plastic hand-gloves, and search in the large dustbins at the back of the house for chicken bones that would later be used for crab fishing. We would record all the large reference books, business handbooks and manuals in Daddy's study in Tshepo's red exercise book and then arrange them in alphabetical order and create library cards for each so that we could monitor their usage. Tshepo was my best friend and I his.

I now wander around the house aimlessly, Tshepo has again vaporised. I cannot think of anything worthwhile I have to do. Although tomorrow is a school day, I have no schoolwork I need to prepare. In fact, I think I am exactly a term ahead of the syllabus. You see, with all the hype around the matric year – that it is the most taxing, the most consequential and a time when you must prove your ability so as to secure yourself a position in a first-class tertiary institution – I had thought it wise to start preparing for the great challenge as early as my grade eleven year. It turns out that all the hype was just exactly that: hype. Using Tshepo's old textbooks, I cruised through the first chapters and found that by Christmas Eve I had already covered half of the year's content before the year even began.

I now walk up to my room. When I get there I will work through past matric examination papers. From fear of completing the entire syllabus and having nothing to do for the rest of the year (and of lack of anything better to do), I had spent the rest of the December vacation working on some previous matric examination papers Tshepo had left in the newspaper room. I loved it. And when those were through, Daddy was only thrilled to buy me a book of past matric examination papers that dated as far back as 1995! The thought that the answers to every question, no matter how challenging, were there at the back of the book in the Answers section was comforting and therapeutic. It was, and I suppose still is, the only thing that is certain in my life. Those sums are the only thing that makes perfect sense. I know that if I ever make a mistake, am ever stuck, unsure of the value of x, find that my books do not balance or that I cannot remember the name of the muscle that raises the upper eyelid, the solution will be there, a few pages away, and then everything will be right again.

I abhor my bedroom. It is a creamy-pink room with a four-poster bed placed in the centre that makes me think of little bald girls dying of cancer. It is a sombre room.

When I was a little younger, a lot more foolish, but nevertheless happier than I am now, I covered my bedroom wall with posters of people I thought were the greatest breathing beings of our time. I remember spending hours one Saturday afternoon, carefully sticking the magazine cut-outs up, mindful to first stick sticky-tape on the back of the silky pages, so that the Prestik would not tear them up if they were ever removed. Exhausted, I lay on my back, admiring the walls, proud of my efforts. Tshepo walked in a little while later, probably wondering where I had disappeared to. I watched his eyes look around; I was excited because I knew I had done a good job.

"Take them down," Tshepo said.

"What?" I asked, irritated at Tshepo's irrationality. Did he not see how much work I had put into this? All he could think about was the expensive paint on the walls.

"Take them down, Ofilwe."

"But Tshepo, look how nice it looks. I promise they won't make the paint peel off. I won't ever move them around." Yeah right, I thought to myself. I'll move them around if I want to. I didn't think he was serious; besides, who was Tshepo to tell me what to do?

The rest that followed was a jumble. A jumble I can barely remember, except for the word 'white'. White. White. White. There was not a single face of colour on the wall. I had not noticed. Honest. It was only after he pointed it out that I saw it too. I mean, why on earth would I do something like that intentionally? What did it matter anyway? It was purely a coincidence; perhaps there were no black faces I liked in the magazines I cut out from. "None at all?" I looked around once more and then at Tshepo. In his eyes I saw what was only to hit me many years from then. I think it was on

*that day that Tshepo saw me for what I was. I wish
I had then too; maybe things would have worked out
differently.*

In every classroom children are dying. It is a parasitic
disease, seizing the mind for its own usage. Using the
mind for its own survival. So that it might grow, divide,
multiply and infect others. Burnt sienna washing out.
DNA coding for white greed, blond vanity and blue-
eyed malevolence. IsiZulu forgotten. Tshivenda a
distant memory.

*"You will find, Ofilwe, that the people you strive so
hard to be like will one day reject you because as much
as you may pretend, you are not one of their own.
Then you will turn back, but there too you will find no
acceptance, for those you once rejected will no longer
recognise the thing you have become. So far, too far to
return. So much, too much you have changed. Stuck
between two worlds, shunned by both."*

I just sit here. I'm done. I am done with doing
calculations. I am through with working out vectors.
For now it is no longer a goal of mine to find answers.
It is what it is. Why try and understand it? The day
is almost done. If I sleep now, the new day will come
sooner, with its own tasks and obligations, and today
will be forgotten.

Part Two

"Promise to keep a secret?"

"What kind of secret?"

"A bad secret."

"Dark?"

"Black."

I watch my clock radio flicker to life. The blinking of the electronic red numerals hurts my eyes, but I squint hard to stop them from closing. The pain will harden them and make them stronger. The blinking is followed by DJ Tinky's husky voice, which enters the early morning stillness like a wisp of smoke. I quickly bury the clock radio under the Lentso Communications sweater I now call my pillow and find the 'off' knob, groping with my sleepy fingers in the darkness. Uncle stirs in the bed next to me. I shut my eyes tight and hold my breath and focus on making my body completely lifeless. I really need to figure out how to get this thing to buzz without switching on the music. I do not want to have to deal with Uncle so early in the morning. Uncle's breathing slows down and soon he is blowing trumpets through his nose again and so I know it is safe to get up. He is fast asleep.

"Oh, I am fortune's fool!" *Uncle would begin, whimpering.*

"Yes, Uncle," I would sigh. No, Uncle, I would think. Not again, not now, please. I had homework to do. Homework I hated, but homework I had to do.

"I have lost all my mirth, the earth seems sterile."

"Yes, Uncle," I would say again, for that was all that was expected from me, the fifteen-year-old niece, during these laments when Uncle would spew out pieces of Shakespeare as if he thought them up himself whilst lost in the abyss of his sorry existence.

"I am dying, Fikile, dying," he would wail, clumsily throwing himself onto the poor old couch and then, as if suddenly becoming aware of the volume of his voice, begin softly whimpering again.

"Yes, Uncle."

"When beggars die, there are no comets seen," he would sob, pulling from his pocket his crumpled handkerchief along with a couple of five-cent pieces that would clink noisily to the ground.

"Yes, Uncle."

"Why me?" he would cry. And I would cry out the same in my head. Why me? Why do I have to listen to Uncle blubber and snivel and sob out garbage every day of my life?

"Yes, Uncle."

"I am a godly man, Fikile."

"Yes, Uncle."

"I am an honest man, Fikile."

"Yes, Uncle."

"A righteous man, Fikile."

"Yes, Uncle."

"That it should come to this?"

"Yes, Uncle"

"I struggle each day to keep a free and open nature."

"Yes, Uncle."

"The world is grown so bad that wrens make prey where eagles dare not perch."

At this point, of course, I had long stopped listening and was writing out my corrections at the back of my test book. I had listened with heartfelt concern the first time he'd come home crying (this was years ago) and taken earnest notice the second time, but by the third or fourth time I realised it made no difference whether I listened or not. He was speaking to himself, and all he wanted me to say was "Yes, Uncle."

"They use me, Fikile."

So what if they used him? He had messed up his own life. He had messed up all the grand opportunities he once had to be something and now some kind white people had been nice enough to give him a job and he had the audacity to complain about it. It didn't matter what the job involved, it wasn't like he was killing people or anything. I had problems of my own. I deplored school and was trying my best to stay out of trouble by doing my corrections like Mrs. Ralefetha had said, but it was difficult to concentrate with the intermittent "Yes, Uncle," I had to say.

"*I mind my own business, Fikile.*"

"*Yes, Uncle.*"

"*I sit in my chair at the security desk and read my books and mind my own business.*"

"*Yes, Uncle.*"

"*I love my books. You know I love my books?*"

"*Yes, Uncle.*"

"*My Hamlet, my kings – Richard and Lear – my Julius Caesar, my Antony and Cleopatra, my beautiful but yet so tragic Romeo and Juliet.*"

"*Yes, Uncle.*"

"*Ah, but some rise by sin and some by virtue fall.*"

"*Yes, Uncle.*" *And there he'd go again, weeping disgracefully.*

"*Oh Fikile, when Mr Dix approached me at my humble security desk and inquired about the books I read, I was only honoured to share with him the might, the mastery and supremacy that lay within those pages.*"

"*Yes, Uncle.*"

"*But he is mad that trusts in the tameness of a*

*wolf, a horse's health, a boy's love or a whore's oath.
I was a fool."*

"Yes, Uncle."

"Was I a fool, Fikile?"

"Yes, Uncle."

"Oh!" he would wail, "You are right, I am a fool!"

*And then I, startled out of my corrections and back
into the sorry reality of the present, would realise that
was one of those moments when I was supposed to
say "No, Uncle" instead of "Yes, Uncle." But there
were few moments like those, so I paid them no mind,
except to quickly rectify things with a "No, Uncle."
Then he would cease wailing and get back to his
whining, which was only slightly less aggravating.*

"No, Uncle."

*"No, you are right, Fikile, I was a fool. I should have
known those heavy white men in their dry-cleaned
suits were not interested in my sonnets but in my black
skin."*

"Yes, Uncle."

*"But how was I to know, Fikile? How was I to know?"
he would ask, his eyes fast filling to the brim, pleading.
Such a twerp, I thought. Such a sorry, pathetic, little
twerp.*

"Oh, *what men dare do! What men may do! What men daily do, not knowing what they do!*"

"Yes, Uncle." I loathed this man.

"What a piece of work man is." He loved this, did Uncle. He loved the backstroke and freestyle in his private soup of sorrow.

"Yes, Uncle."

"It is a curse, Fikile, to have a heart as big as mine."

"Yes, Uncle."

"Today we went to Hyde Park, to the offices of Borman-Nkosinathi. Tall buildings, glass doors."

"Yes, Uncle."

"They dressed me up in a brown suit with yellow lines. I chuckled to myself as I put it on in our security officer's box. Me, in a brown suit with yellow lines, Fikile! I looked like a real Sexwale!"

"Yes, Uncle."

"But all that glitters is not gold," he whispered, his thick lower lip trembling.

"Yes, Uncle."

"We drove in Mr Dix's car and I sat in the front seat."

"Yes, Uncle."

"I always sit in the front seat on the way to the meetings and in the back seat when I am sent home."

"Yes, Uncle."

"He said, Mr Dix, he said that he was very proud of me and that I should be proud of myself, too. He said he wished more of the employees could be like me and show such loyalty to the company."

"Yes, Uncle."

"I laughed to myself, Fikile, sitting there in the front seat of Mr Dix's Jaguar. It was really me! And Mr Dix, the CEO of Lentso Communications, was telling me that he was very proud of me and that he wished more employees could be more like me. Ha! Imagine that!"

"Yes, Uncle."

"But then when we arrived at Borman-Nkosinathi and were getting out of the car, he took me aside and said that it would probably be better if I did not speak at the meeting that day. I was dismayed at that because, well, I don't know if you know, but I do like to speak very much. But nevertheless, what can one say? The boss had spoken."

"Yes, Uncle."

"*He said they would once again introduce me as Silas Nyoni, their Black Economic Empowerment partner, and newly appointed Operations Manager of Lentso Communications. Today's plan was that Laurie, Mr Dix's personal assistant, would rush in during the meeting with Borman-Nkosinathi and say that I was urgently needed at the offices. Then I would be hurried out and taken back to my security box. I imagine they were afraid I would say something senseless that would give them away, so Mr Dix signalled to Laurie earlier than planned and I was rushed out soon after the introductions.*"

"*Yes, Uncle.*"

"*I would not have said something senseless, Fikile. I do not know why they think these things about me. I would never do anything to jeopardise Lentso Communications! That company is my bread and butter.*"

"*Yes, Uncle.*"

"*I managed to steal a brief look at the agenda for the meeting, Fikile, and there were some pretty compelling topics on there. I deem if they had given me half the chance, let me stay just a little while, I might have been able to add something useful, something salutary, to their discussion.*"

"*Yes, Uncle.*"

"*Of course they only think of me as a security guard.*

But there's things about me those white men do not know, Fikile. And I just think sometimes that maybe if I spoke up, said something profound or gave an insightful suggestion, then maybe they'd see that there's more to the security officer than black skin and Shakespeare. Maybe they'd see that I belong in that brown suit with yellow stripes."

"Yes, Uncle."

"In my mind's eye, I am Silas Nyoni."

"Yes, Uncle."

"But they see nothing." He'd say this with such despair that I might have felt sorry for him if I didn't know better.

"Yes, Uncle."

"Laurie made me take off the suit in the back seat, Fikile. How does a grown man such as myself undress like a child in the back seat of a car?"

"Yes, Uncle."

"And then they give me another radio and a pat on the back as if I were some circus animal, rewarded for performing a clever trick. If it wasn't for me, Fikile – me, Silas Nyoni – they would never be making the deals I am making for them. Those white men don't realise that I am compromising my moral beliefs to make them billions. One day they'll lose me and they'll be sorry."

I did not respond this time. I was afraid if I opened my mouth I would retch. If he resented the job so much why didn't he simply stop doing it? 'Oh, I'm a godly man, Fikile.' Sniff-sniff. 'Just trying to live an honest life, Fikile.' Sniff-sniff. 'I am a man more sinned against than sinning.' Sniff-sniff. Bullshit. Absolute bullshit! Uncle knew very well that from that first day when Mr Dix asked him to read him passages from his books and asked him to recite the poetry, Uncle lauded over everyone; he was being interviewed, assessed and evaluated for the position of black fake senior partner/CEO/co-founder/financial director or whatever position it was that spoke of transformation at Lentso Communications.

Uncle reads the papers. In fact, Uncle reads more papers than most! This whole thing of using nameless black faces as pawns for striking black economic empowerment deals was nothing new and he knew it. He delighted in it. The man celebrated it! Sweet, gentle Uncle with the 'world's biggest heart' was no security guard: he'd weep right through any break-in. No, Uncle loved the soft life, yearned for the soft life, lived for the soft life, just like everyone else. He revelled in those moments when he'd be wearing striped suits and sit in the front seat while Laurie sat in the back. Uncle was just another hungry black man, hungry for a piece of the pie just like the rest of us.

But what infuriated me and drove me absolutely out of my mind with indignation was that Uncle wanted to eat his pie and then have us feel sorry for him because it was making him fat. Uncle is a liar and a fake. He dotes on his new position as fake black bigshot of

Lentso Communications. He knows very well it's all he's good for. Hell, he should be grateful for such an opportunity! Not everybody gets a second shot at the good life. He is pathetic as a security guard and probably would have been fired by now if they hadn't found out that he spoke English so well. He should be bloody grateful, the bloody twit.

I am relieved that the time for sleep is over and I am already thinking about all the great happenings that today may have in store. Waking up is always a thrilling time for me because it presents a new and fresh chance at life filled with endless possibilities. Sleep is an unnecessary luxury and I generally do what I can to avoid it. In sleep you lose all control and are vulnerable to the many monsters of the night. In sleep you waste precious hours that may have been used to plan great things and make purposeful strides towards your dreams, like my Project Infinity. Only infants and senile people really need sleep. The rest are simple, weak and lazy.

I am glad it is time again to leave this hole. I have been possessed by a spirit of vigour in the night and today will go out filled with courage and determination, my mind attentive for any opportunity that may come my way. Perhaps today will be the day, that day, the one I will call 'the day my life turned around', the one I will look back at when I am rich and famous living in Project Infinity and laugh and shake my head and take a sip of a frozen martini and think to myself, 'Did you ever imagine it would be like this?' I have not a cent in the bank nor very much of an education, but a heart so heavy with ambition that it may just fall to the depths of my stomach if Project Infinity is not realised.

Yes, I have been weak and lazy of late, feeling tired and crying into my pillow. But all that has come to an end now and I am officially back in the game. I have realised that there is no gain in feeling sorry for oneself, it really is a shameful thing to do, common to the likes of Uncle, who sit and nap their lives away and then cry into the night expecting the rest of us to comfort them as if they did not bring their wretched states upon themselves.

I knew in advance when it was going to happen. I could tell because Uncle would always have that sorry look on his face when he came back home from work. I'd be sitting on the kitchen floor still in my school uniform writing out my mathematics or practising my English readings when I would hear him dragging his feet through the dirt past the Tshabalala's house to our one-bedroom hovel at the end of the Tshabalala's garden.

Ous Joy, Mr. Tshabalala's eldest daughter, would squeal her usual "Very good evening to you, Uncle, and you are how today?" from their kitchen window, hoping that the man she'd flirted with for years would say more than his usual "Very well, my sweet Joy, very well. Good night, good night! Parting is such sweet sorrow." But on those evenings when it happened, Uncle would not respond to his sweet Joy, whom he also secretly admired. He never had the guts to do anything about it in fear of Mr. Tshabalala's quick temper. On those nights when it happened he'd simply nod a sad hello to her and pass.

Of course there was always the chance that I had not heard his "Very well, my sweet Joy, very well. Good night, good night! Parting is such sweet sorrow," so I would close my books, clear the floor and stand facing the front door so I could see what kind of expression he had on his face when he walked in. And if it was that sorry look... that sorry, pathetic 'Oh, woe is me' look, then I would know that tonight would be one of those nights when it would happen.

I would try to cheer him up. I would try to cheer him up with all my might. I would run and take his bags and hurriedly return with his worn slippers in my hand. I later realised that the look of those tattered slippers at his feet intensified his doleful mood so I took to returning with his weekend push-ins instead. I would shout with glee, "Uncle, we sang your flavourite song at assembly today." And then I would sing, "Jesus loves me, yes I know, floor the bible tells me so!" And while I sang with all the enthusiasm my little body could muster, I would open up my school books and show him each "Well done, Fikile" and "Excellent, Fikile!" that I had forged on every other page. And when it seemed as if I might be losing him, I would begin to recite the Our Father: "Our Farther who heart in heaven, hello be thire name," because it always pleased Uncle to hear me say it and roll the r's the way he liked them.

But it seldom worked. When Uncle had that sorry, pathetic look on his face, there was very little that one could do to make him feel any better. Uncle would look down at me as I knelt at his feet smiling and laughing and screaming Hallelujahs whilst I undid his shoelaces and then he would sigh a very deep and desolate sigh and shuffle towards our bedroom.

But of course I would not give up. I would not allow his regretful state to discourage me. I would stretch my little arms up and onto his back and then march him around the room, away from the bedroom door, singing, "Oh, when the saints! Oh, when the saints! Oh when the saints coming marching in... I want to be in that mamba, oh when the saints come marching in!" I would push at his back, marching and stomping my little feet with all the stompingness that they had in them, throwing my tiny voice up into the heavens.

But when Uncle had that sorry, pathetic look on his face, there was very little that one could do to make him feel any better. I would hear Uncle begin to sniffle. Even through the hymns that bellowed from my little chest, I would hear Uncle sniffle. Even when I sang louder than I had ever sung before, I would still hear that sniffle, and then I would know I was defeated. Even though I marched a mean march with ardour and devotion and pushed at his giant back with every muscle I owned, Uncle would not budge. The intervals between the sniffling would grow shorter, and soon his whole body would begin to shudder. Uncle would turn around and look at me, as if not quite sure what I was. Then, recollecting, he would sigh that weighty sigh and slowly the water level in his eyes would rise until it spilled over, making him *hurriedly shuffle his sorry self into our bedroom and under the covers.*

All the performing – the marching and singing and laughing and clapping – generally wore me out, but on those days that it happened, I would try my utmost to stay up as late as I possibly could. It was a silly hope of mine that Uncle would be blowing trumpets through his nose by the time I climbed into our bed. Because although on the days it happened Uncle spent most of the time lying in our bed, he very rarely fell asleep. Of course I would try my absolute best to stay up, sometimes as late as ten o'clock, but it was always only a matter of time until my spelling words were sliding up the page.

Our bedroom would be quiet when I crept in but as soon as I huddled into the corner of the bed I would hear his pathetic sniffling followed by the sorry sigh. It was only a single bed, so when Uncle would turn his massive form to face me, I'd be stripped of the thin covers that were my only protection. Uncle would always begin with, "Oh, Fikile, why must life be so hard?" which would be followed by a "What did we do, Fikile, to deserve such pain?"

I never did answer him and I don't think he ever expected me to. Uncle would then take my little hand and gently slip it into the loose tracksuit pants he wore at night. Uncle was always gentle. In fact, people often would say, "Oh Uncle, he's such a gentle man. Not a single violent bone in him." But the snake inside Uncle's pants was always awake. It was always hot

113

and rubbery and would sometimes stick to the palm of my hand as Uncle moved my hand up and down it. It was always at this point that Uncle would begin to sob, first slightly, as if only for himself, and then louder and louder, moving my hand faster and faster and harder, until he cried out in agony for all the world to hear. Then he would fall asleep, blowing trumpets through his nose.

I hated that Uncle was such a sorry and pathetic and weak man and hated even more that I was the only one who was able to comfort him. But I had to admit to myself that my own lack of discipline could have been at fault. In the few years I lived with Uncle, I never found another way to comfort him. I thus spent my afternoons once school was out reading the easy words in Uncle's set of encyclopaedias, hoping to impress him one day with all my knowledge when I had learnt to read the bigger words too. I was hoping that in that way I might keep him happy. But it never worked.

Back then, when I was very young, I actually sort of liked Uncle, especially when he was in a happy mood. Uncle had always been kind to me. He never hit me like my mother used to, and he often brought home sweets whenever they were selling them on the train. After my mother slit her wrists and let her blood spill all over me, right until I was soaked through to my skin as I slept against the hollow of her stomach, Uncle was the only one who was willing to take me in. Gogo, my granny, had too many of her own white children to take care of and my father had run off long before I had even implanted into my mother's womb.

114

So to me, back then anyway, Uncle was a pretty good guy. Ja, he had his bad qualities like most people, but he was Uncle, the only real family I had.

But then again, I was only a child and didn't know any better. It was only in grade seven, after those Childline Ousies had come to our school and talked to us about rape, that things changed between Uncle and me. Uncle had never touched me in a bad way and all I had ever done was rub his snake when he was sad to stop him from crying. But the Childline Ousies had said all this stuff about private parts and how they were private and that it is not your fault and that you should call someone. I had gotten so confused and muddled in my head that I had to be sent to sick bay because I had started throwing up right there on the assembly floor.

That evening Uncle came home with that sorry, pathetic look on his face again, shuffling his feet and sighing. I was still feeling quite queasy, so this time did not try to sing and jump and laugh and stomp as I often did, but instead I sat on the kitchen floor doing division and drinking lots of fluids as Madam Teacher had advised. I did stay up late that night, though. But when I crept into our bedroom I was suddenly overtaken by the notion to sleep on the floor and not get into the bed where Uncle was waiting for me to comfort him.

I slept on the hard cement floor that night without the protection of any covers and slept like that the night after and the night after that. Uncle didn't blow trumpets out of his nose once that night, but never said a word about the new sleeping arrangement. He stopped bringing me home sweets when they sold them on the train, though, but I realised I never really did like those sweets all that much.

I gather myself up from the floor. My back no longer protests like it used to when I first traded in my space next to Uncle on the bed for the hard cement on the floor. It's actually not all that bad. I use old sweaters as pillows and in the winter sleep in three or four layers of clothing. I have been sleeping on this floor for five years now. Thirteen, fourteen, fifteen, sixteen, seventeen, eighteen… yes, five years since that night I decided it was not my responsibility to lull Uncle to sleep by rubbing his dick. And now it is only my neck that continues to groan and moan, the rest of my body has gotten quite used to the floor. Of course, things will not be this way forever. Someday I will own a king-sized bed with a solid-wood headboard dressed in decorative ironwork and red leather with a large foot-end kist filled with little gold cushions and decadent fabrics. And even though I do not really believe in sleep, I will still cover it with lots of soft and cosy blankets and white and fluffy pillows because it will be mine and I will have the money to do so. It really is only a matter of time until I'm out of this hole, gone and gone for good, never to return again.

I drag my box from under the bed and take out my work clothes. Our uniform is plain and indistinct and so I have painted my fingernails a cherry red to set me apart as I seat customers, collect plates, pour glasses of sparkling water and delicately run my fingers along the tops of chairs. Every morning I make sure that I top up any nail-polish chips or cracks that may have developed overnight because I have come to know the great importance of presentation.

Everything that matters to me is in this box. I have a shelf in Uncle's cupboard that keeps some old stuff I hardly ever use any more like my school uniform and some ragged shoes that I have not worn in years, but in the box lie my life's treasures. My magazines, all of them, from the first *Glossy* I read when I was thirteen, to this month's issue of *Girlfriend*, are in the box. Beside them is my contact lens case, holding within the most expensive things I own, worth many months spent scrubbing grease and sweeping storerooms after hours. The dainty little emerald-green coloured lenses that float gracefully in the sapphire blue contact-lens solution are a reminder of how far I have come, from the naive orphan child living in a one-bedroom house with her incompetent Uncle in another family's back-yard in yet another decrepit township to the charming young waitress with pretty green eyes and soft, blow-in-the-wind, caramel-blond hair (pinned in perfectly to make it look real), working at the classiest coffee shop this side of the equator. My Lemon Light skin-lightener cream, my sunscreen, my eyeliner, mascara, eye-shadow, blush, eyelash-straightener and the pieces of caramel-blond hair extension which were bought for me as a child to braid my hair with but never used because Uncle misplaced the money he was supposed to pay the braiding lady with, are all little testimonies to the progress I have made despite the odds. They are hard evidence of how much closer I am to Project Infinity.

I take out the green gems, my eyelash-straightener, my foundation, my Berry Liscious lipstick and my clothes from the box and take them into the kitchen where I will bathe and dress. We do not have a bath or an inside toilet like the Tshabalalas do or like some of the more advanced homes in Mphe Batho Township, so I have to collect water from the taps outside, boil it and clean myself in a bucket in the kitchen. Perhaps if Uncle spent less time crying and more time finding ways to capitalise on his new position as fake black economic empowerment partner, then maybe we could afford to instal a toilet or even a bath in our home. But perhaps it is for the better that the conditions in this dump never improve. They can serve as a constant reminder to me of what I do not want to be: black, dirty and poor. This bucket can be a daily motivator for me to keep me working towards where I will someday be: white, rich and happy. You see, that's the difference between Uncle and me and in fact between me and most of the hopeless, shortsighted people in Mphe Batho. I know what I want in life and am prepared to do anything in my power to get it.

Am I going crazy? Am I already crazy? No. Maybe. Maybe crazy is what you need to be to get somewhere in life. Like those inventors or whatever who created aeroplanes and things; didn't everyone think they were crazy when they said they wanted to fly? And now look, everyone's flying. If crazy is what I need to be to get out of here and into Project Infinity, then crazy is what I am going to be.

I proudly set my Silver Spoon uniform – the black tight-fitting jeans and the black T-shirt with a silver spoon running down its back – out on the red-and-white-checkered plastic kitchen table that Gogo bought for Uncle when he first moved into this place many years ago, before I was even born. The T-shirts were given to us by the coffee shop, but the jeans we had to purchase ourselves. At the time, it being my first job, and having recently dropped out of high school on a whim with no money and no means of making any, I did not know how I was going to get my hands on a pair of black jeans and nearly lost the job for showing up at work twice 'incorrectly attired'. But I soon pulled myself together and made a plan. There was no way a single pair of silly jeans was going to stand in the way of me and Project Infinity. Sometimes in life you have to push the boundaries, be creative, stretch your resources and take the road less travelled to get what you want.

"Fiks, dear, we love you, you know that."

"Yes, Miss Becky." Had she said she loved me? Miss Becky loved me? They loved me?

"Dahling, you are gorgeous. So well spoken, so bright, just to die for."

"Yes, Miss Becky." It had only been two weeks at this new job and they loved me. I could not believe it.

I mean, I knew I was brilliant at anything I set my mind on doing, but it's so different when you hear it in somebody else's words.

"But you see, dahling, I am going to be very blunt with you now. Silver Spoon is an upmarket establishment. Top notch. Right up there on the food chain. We have a reputation, sweetheart, a loyal clientele. Dahling, do you see the people who walk through our doors? Do you actually see the people we serve? Well, do you?"

"Yes, Miss Becky." Her tone had changed and I was getting a little frightened.

"The people who come here, sweetheart, are respectable people. Dignified and accomplished people. Do you understand that, dahling?"

"Yes, Miss Becky."

"The people we have here, dear, are great politicians, businessmen and judges, Fiks. They are the people who make this country. Without them, well, you and I wouldn't even be having this conversation, would we?"

"Yes, Miss Becky."

That last comment made her laugh, a strange and awkward laugh. I did not laugh with her, although I probably should have. I was too busy frantically trying to figure out where this conversation was going and what the most appropriate response would be.

"Well dahling, what I am getting at is that the very least we can do is to give these hard-working people the class that they deserve, the class that they pay for when they come here, the class that Silver Spoon Coffee Shop promises to always deliver. And with you incorrectly attired, dressed like that, dahling, wearing our Silver Spoon T-shirt over those murky brown trousers, well, I don't see how the two could possibly ever work."

"But…"

"No 'buts', dear."

I wanted to explain that I understood the uniform requirements perfectly and I was working on buying a pair of black jeans. I had even gone up the yard to the Tshabalalas, whom I deplored because they thought they were better than us, to try see if Ous Joy, who was the only Tshabalala I could stand, might have a pair of black jeans I could borrow for the meantime. I had spoken to Uncle about lending me some money to buy a pair and had assured him that I would pay him back with my wages as soon as I had them. But Uncle had no money and said that I needed to wait until month end. Of course that wouldn't work because month end was a long way away. But I was working on a plan D and just needed a little bit of time.

"Yes, Miss Becky."

"You have until tomorrow, sweetie. Make a plan. Gosh, it's a fucking pair of jeans, not a pair of Jimmy

121

Choo shoes. And that hair, dear, do something about it, anything, just don't come to work looking like that again."

"Yes, Miss Becky."

I walked out of Silver Spoon that afternoon straight into The Meisies Store across the way. My heart was thumping against my rib cage, each breath hurtling out of my flared nostrils in short, forced bits. I could hear the blood rushing past my ears. I refused to lose this job. And so when I got onto the escalator and headed down, first past the lingerie section and then the fragrances, I knew what I had to do. I calmly removed from the shelf the first size 32 black jeans I saw, folded them into my bag and went back up the escalator, past the fragrances and then the lingerie section and walked out of the store.

I fill my bathing bucket with boiling water and switch on the kitchen radio. Radios, radios everywhere, on every shelf, in every corner, packed up in boxes and stacked in piles. All of them gifts from Lentso Communications, thank-yours for all the perjury and forgery Uncle does for them. Uncle is an idiot and they know it. All he'd have to do is ask them for money and they'd give it to him, they know how much power he has with the information he holds and how he could annihilate them if he told someone about the actual terms of his employment. But do you think Uncle would ever work up the balls to ask for enough for even just his taxi-fare back home? No. Why? Because Uncle is a first-grade dimwit. He sincerely believes that they hired him for his intellect. Ha! Intellect? They hired Uncle because he's got *Yes-Man* written all over his face.

I remember how as a child I would page through the photo albums of Uncle growing up at the Kinsleys. I would stare for what must have been hours at each individual photo and then close my eyes and try to picture myself in them. Me, instead of Uncle. There was one photo I particularly liked. It was of Uncle's ninth birthday party and at the time I was nine years old, too. I had never had a birthday party in my life. I didn't even know of anyone who had had a birthday party. Uncle sat in the centre of a large table of crisps and Fizzers and Cheese Curls and Smarties and little round colourful chewing gums and paper cups filled with Coke and Fanta and purple juice and a large multicoloured cake with nine blue and white candles. There was a red and yellow jumping castle in the background and children everywhere. White children *everywhere. Some of them were jumping, some running around, some playing in the pool and others sitting with Uncle at the table, smiling for the camera. Smiling for Uncle.* White children smiling *for Uncle! I remember being filled with such wild envy and rage that I was unable to understand why that couldn't be me in the photo, why the Kinsleys hadn't thrown such a party for me, why nobody had ever thrown any kind of party for me. I got my blunt-nose scissors out of my school bag and cut that photo into a gazillion tiny pieces, put them in my mouth and chewed them all up. Uncle didn't deserve any of that.*

Uncle could have had it all and he screwed it up. The Kinsleys did so much for Uncle even though they didn't have to. I mean, he was only their domestic worker's son and yet they treated him like he was one of their own. Those poor, poor Kinsleys. If only they had known that all that money they were investing in tuition, school uniforms, piano lessons and expensive encyclopaedias would one day go to waste. If only they had invested that money in me instead of Uncle. I knew I was clever, more clever than Uncle would ever be and more grateful. I knew that if I was given half the chance Uncle had been given, I would never have turned out to be a disappointment. No, unlike Uncle I would have been grateful for an opportunity at a better life.

Sometimes Gogo got into the mood of telling stories about 'those filthy homes of those rich white people' which she spent most of her days cleaning and when she did I would sit still and listen carefully, waiting for the part where she would get to talking about the Kinsleys. She didn't have very much to say about them because they weren't as cruel and cold-blooded as the others. My grandmother hated speaking about the good white people, so she would often only say a word or two about the Kinsley family and their home. Gogo would grumble a little about how she didn't understand why the Kinsleys had chosen to only pay for Uncle's schooling when Charmin (my mother) was just as smart. Then she'd grouch a bit more about how white people enjoyed breaking up black families.

One day I gently asked Gogo if she still remembered where the Kinsleys lived and what their address was.

I was certain that if I could go there just once – let them see me just once – then they'd immediately recognise that I was much more clever than Uncle and a much more worthwhile investment. I knew that if I was given the chance to meet the Kinsleys, then all my problems would be solved, for they would surely ask me to move into their home right then and there and change my name to something cute like Sarah Kinsley. Gogo had looked at me over her glasses for a long time with a frown on her face. I think maybe she thought that I wanted to go over there and steal from them or something crazy, which was really ridiculous because I was only nine or ten at the time, but Gogo always worried that my mother's blood had cursed me and it was only a matter of time until I ended up in jail or dead. So Gogo ignored my question and moved on to the Samuelses and how they used to give her Mrs Samuels's old underwear as a Christmas present.

I'd known Uncle was an idiot even before Gogo told me his story. Like I said, I was a gifted child, and could see right through his fancy English and mounds of books. Gogo's version of Uncle's fall simply confirmed the suspicions I had held since the age of five or something. My own personal interpretation of what really happened is that Uncle had allowed living with the Kinsleys to get to his head. The Sunday lunches on their patio, Mrs Kinsley with a large straw hat on and the boys helping Mr Kinsley at the braai, the bicycle with blue training wheels and the birthday parties every year. All those white children smiling for Uncle, singing for Uncle, dancing and playing for Uncle, messed with his head and loosened a few screws.

If it had been me, I would have kept my cool. I would have taken it in my stride. I would have taken it a day at a time. But Uncle gobbled it all up at once. The cake, the Fizzers, the Cheese Curls, the purple juice, the bedroom with blue walls and Spiderman sheets, the holidays at the dam and all those smiling white faces he swallowed at once, without chewing.

Nobody really knows what exactly went awry in his head because as the story goes Uncle just came home after his first semester at the University of Cape Town with a letter of exclusion from the medical school in his bookbag. He was fat and crying into the pillow he took with him to Cape Town when the entire family waved him goodbye at the bus station at the beginning of that year. He lay in bed for weeks sobbing and eating whatever Gogo put at his door and that was the end of it, the end of Uncle the smart one, the one who spoke the white man's language, the one who would save us.

Gogo told me that some blamed it on the Kinsleys, that they had seen a capable young black boy and thought it their right to remove him from his home and his people in the township where he belonged and whisk him off to their thatch-roofed house in the suburbs where they confused him with their white this or that and then dropped him when he crumbled in the real world. Nonsense, I thought. I knew better than to give my opinion, and sat quietly and listened on. Others believed that Uncle had simply grown too big for his boots. He'd outgrown not only his boots, they had said, but his black skin.

Uncle had grown proud. He had forgotten who he was and where he came from and as a result had been punished by the gods. Of course he could be forgiven, they said, if only he performed the correct rituals, but everybody knew that Uncle no longer believed in them. Others secretly suggested that it was Gogo's fault for not performing the necessary thanksgiving ceremonies when he was sent off, or for allowing him to stay with the Kinsleys in the first place, or for allowing him to go to university and not encouraging him to work like other men.

There were many theories but I thought all of them were a huge heap of crap. Uncle failed dismally and was excluded from the medical school at the University of Cape Town because he was an idiot. Simple. Uncle was an idiot and got what idiots got. He probably didn't study for any of the tests because he idiotically thought he was too smart to study. Absolute idiot. Gogo was upset because the Kinsleys didn't even try to do anything about it, it was as if they had never known him, raised him, pushed him to study further and be a doctor. They didn't call or write or anything, just went on with their lives and weekends away fishing at the dam and a few years later emigrated to Australia.

But what should the poor people have done? They had paid for him all the way through the second part of primary school and high school and then were even prepared to pay for his way through medical school. What more, really, could the poor people do? It wasn't their fault that Uncle was an idiot. Trust black people to complain when white people don't do anything *to help them and then complain when they do and then complain when they don't help them again after they've screwed it up. If I were the Kinsleys I would have made Uncle pay me back for all the money I invested in his empty head, with interest.*

"You are listening to the twilight zone with me DJ Tinky on this beautiful Sunday morning. A brand new day! New beginnings! Another shot! What are you crazy people doing up so early! Call us and tell us why you aren't in bed, Joburg!"

I eat a slice of bread with coffee and make porridge for Uncle. I don't know why I do it. He is a grown man and should be able to make his own breakfast. But I will do it today because I have time. Whether I do it tomorrow will depend on how I feel. The idiot does not deserve it.

As I leave the house DJ Tinky plays *Fast Car* by Tracy Chapman. Weird woman, sounds like a man. It makes me feel funny, sort of scared and excited at the same time. I haven't heard the song in years. 'New beginnings' huh, DJ Tinky? 'Another shot?' Well, let's hope you are right.

You'd be surprised how full the train station can get on a Sunday. I avoid the groups of noisy people and sit on the edge of a bench next to a little girl too young to try to strike up conversation with me and pull out my *Girlfriend* magazine from my handbag. I do not know why people here have taken upon themselves the duty of making attempts at speaking to me. I work hard to keep the 'don't speak to me' look on my face and yet it seems they read it as 'please speak to me'. It is especially bad on a Sunday because the trains are unreliable and come round every hour if they do at all, so people seem to think striking random conversations with strangers is a good way of killing time.

It really is very inconsiderate. Sometimes one just wants to be alone with one's thoughts and not have to deal with bad breath and body odour so early in the morning. Women are not so bad. They bore me with their questions about how I manage to keep my figure so slim or the stories about their harsh white bosses at work or the long tales of their various illnesses, aches and pains, but I still prefer them to the men. The men disgust me. All of them are a bunch of criminals. A bunch of uneducated criminals. They look at me like they want to rape me and I know they would do it if there weren't so many people around. They call me *Nice* and *Nana* and whisper other crude things as I walk past them hanging against the wall, unclean and smelling of alcohol. I hate them and they know it. They have no respect for women, so why should I have any respect for them? I do not respond to them, even to the ones who greet me politely. I keep my chin up and walk straight past them as if I cannot hear them.

129

Maybe there are some good ones who really mean no harm but unfortunately their peers have sullied their name. In fact, as a general rule I try not to mix with any black men at all. It just makes things easier.

One of the Wimpy girls who thought it a clever idea to befriend me until I put her straight used to warn me that some day the men would grow fed up with my 'snaaks-ness' and I would be made to regret it. But I didn't care, they didn't intimidate me. Besides, what is the point? I will not be living in this dingy old township forever, so why build relationships with people I have no intention of ever seeing again? I want nothing to do with this dirt. Not ever. Not ever in my life again. And I think the people here at the station know it. That's why the Pick 'n Pay ladies look at me the way they do.

"I came into this world alone and I am going to leave it alone, so what is the point?"

"But everybody needs friends, Fikile, even you, my sweetie. Go play outside with the other girls."

"I am fine here with you, Gogo."

"Fikile, I am not fine here with you. Gogo needs some time alone to rest and you need to spend more time with people your own age."

"I will be quiet, Gogo, I won't disturb you."

"Fikile, Uncle and I will not be here forever and then who will you have as company?"

"Myself. I will have myself."

"I am not asking you, I am telling you: go play outside with the other girls."

"But they are stupid, Gogo. They spend the whole day at Sammy's Tavern talking about boys and laughing with old men so that they will buy them cold drinks."

"Then play with other girls, Fikile."

"They are all the same."

"'They are all the same', 'they are boring', 'they can't speak English', 'they are stupid', 'they steal my stuff'. You always have an excuse, Fikile. I am fed up with you sitting in here all day reading those fashion magazines. I have a good mind to take those magazines away from you. I thought that they would be a fine way for you to practise your reading but they have taught you nothing but to be a snob. Go outside and play."

"Take the magazines away, I don't care."

"Fikile! O nyaka ke go bethe ka tlelapa ne? Get outside now."

"It's hot outside and my skin will get dark."

"Fikile, go."

"No."

The man sitting next to me on the train tells me that it is a belief of his that one must always get to know the person you are seated next to when you embark on any sort of journey. I roll my eyes and pretend I do not know that the freak is speaking to me and continue to page through my *Girlfriend*. I watch him out of the corner of my eye as he bends forward to pull his mahogany-brown leather briefcase up from the floor. I notice the padded leather handle, the two classic nickel buckles, the slide latch behind the front buckles, the parallel stitching with thick maroon cotton, and when he flips the front flap open, the V&CX symbols embroidered in red across its inner silk lining. Classy, I think to myself.

He unzips its sides, revealing only a green apple inside which rolls out and down the cabin as he attempts to raise the briefcase up to his lap. He looks as if he is about to go after it, but then changes his mind. It is too far and the train too full. "I was going to offer you some of my apple," he chuckles as he zips up the very expensive-looking briefcase, "but I guess it was never meant to be."

"I have my own food," I reply crisply as I notice the name 'K.J. Fishwick' engraved into the corner of the briefcase. A thief! I think to myself. Typical, I should have known better than to think some garrulous train-riding black man would walk around with a V&CX briefcase he bought for himself.

"So you can talk," he responds, smiling.

I do not look at this man, this man who is a thief like all the other men in this train, and probably an alcoholic and a rapist too. I shift back in my seat, straighten up my back, raise my magazine so it is closer to my eyes and begin to hum lightly, flipping through the pages, while working hard to keep the 'piss off' look on my face.

"The way you read it so intensely, it must be a very good magazine. May I see it?" He snatches my precious *Girlfriend* out of my hand. The bloody nerve! Who is this man and why does he not just leave me alone? "Oh so you're one of those," he says mockingly, looking at the photograph of Avril Lavigne on the cover of the magazine.

"One of what?" I snap back, irritated with this man who thinks he can be so familiar with me.

"You know, those *abo mabhebeza* who are always wishing to be something that they ain't never gonna be." He chuckles.

I do not know who he thinks he is or who he thinks I am, him in his yellowing shirt, worn, stiff and rigid from too much washing, bleaching and ironing. "You have me all sussed out, don't you, Mr. K.J. Fishwick? That is your name, right? Or are *you* one of those thieving black men who just can't keep their hands off white men's property?"

He stares back at me in disbelief.

"Which poor white man did you steal that pretty little briefcase from, Mr Fishwick?" I ask, as I pull the magazine from his grasp.

He does not respond. He just sighs, shakes his head and slips the briefcase behind his feet and underneath his seat. He turns away and looks out of the window for the rest of the ride. Good. I am glad I have my peace and quiet back.

Five more stops until I get off the train, and then I will take a taxi from Sizanani Station and then I will finally be at work. The train trip into the suburbs is always the hardest part of my day to get through. The carriages stink of labourers' sweat and of urine and soaked sanitary towels that should have been changed days ago. It is especially bad in the afternoons on the way back home from work, but it is pretty awful in the mornings too. It makes you wonder if half the people in this train even bother to take a bath before they leave their shacks in the mornings. It really is pure disregard for the rest of us who have to try to stomach these offensive body odours. It is an absence of self-respect too, because no self-respecting person, regardless of circumstance, would walk around smelling the way these people do.

I am anxious to get out of this train and onto the taxi and to work. The train is moving slower than usual today, which is frustrating. Perhaps it has something to do with those cable thefts. Black people! Why must they always be so damn destructive? And to think, they have never invented a thing in their squalid lives and yet they insist on destroying the little we have. Just look at how scummy the townships are. Have you ever seen any white suburb looking so despicable? In some townships it is difficult to differentiate the yards from the garbage heaps. It really is a disgrace, a paucity of perspective.

"And you, Fikile, what do you want to be when you grow up?"

"White, Teacher Zola. I want to be white."

"You so stupid, Fikile, don't you know you going to be as black as dirt for the rest of your life! Tell her Mrs Zola, tell her she's going to be as black as dirt forever."

"Shut up, Ntombana. Mrs Zola said we can grow up to be anything our hearts desire."

"But Fikile, dear, you can't change the colour of your skin. What I meant is that you can –"

"See, Fikile! You so stupid!"

"Ntombana, if you don't keep quiet now I am going to have to send you out of my class."

"I will be white if I want to be white. I don't care what anybody thinks."

"But why would you want to do that, dear?"

"Because it's better."

"What makes you think that, Fikile?"

"Everything."

It is after seven o'clock when we get to Sizanani Station. The people here dress and look a tad better than the ones at home and are not nearly as noisy. I think it might be because they are closer to the suburbs and are thus familiar with the way of life. There are no endless queues at the taxi rank today because it is a Sunday and not even eight o'clock yet, so many people are still fast asleep. I choose a crimson taxi with polished wheels and *First Class* spray-painted on its back window. There is no such thing as a first-class taxi, but I often take this one if it is not too full. It is better than riding in *Desire* or *Yizo Yizo*. I guess it also feels good pretending I really am travelling first class, because someday I will only travel *first class*.

Inside, I spot a seat next to a large woman who sleeps with her head against the window. Her greasy hair makes ugly smudges on the glass as her head slides up and down in sync with her breathing. On her lap sits a skinny little boy with his thumb in his mouth who also looks as if he, too, is well on his way to dreamland. So, because they are both sleeping or at least she is and he soon will be, I decide it's safe to sit next them.

I have begun to believe that there has been a change in me. I am now more confident in everything I do and am no longer uncertain of my capabilities. Nothing intimidates me. I have even started speaking in the English language even when I do not need to. I am no longer concerned with what I sound like because I have come to believe that I sound like any other English-speaking person. I use words like 'facetious' and 'filial' in everyday speech and speak English boldly, without hesitation. Not like Uncle, who spews out fragments of Shakespeare that make little sense to him or anyone else, but with true insight and understanding. There is this new drive that has taken charge of me: it urges me to take command and create my own destiny. I am certain of where I am going and know exactly what it is I want out of life. I have worked hard to be where I am and have little tolerance for those who get in my way.

"Lady!" I yell into her ear, after attempts at nudging her awake have failed.

"Lady, you are going to have to tell your kid to get off me!" I shout again, hoping she will awake and remove the boy.

She turns her head and opens her eyes. "We are here?" she asks, looking out of the window and then around the taxi, confused.

"No, we have not arrived yet, but I would like you to detach your son from my shoulder, please, he is making me very uncomfortable."

She looks at me and then at her boy who lies with his head on my shoulder, his drool and sweat steadily dampening my Silver Spoon T-shirt. She smiles a dopey smile that tells me that her mind is still asleep even though her eyes are awake. "Yes, he is very tired." She says, slurring the words. "We are very tired, we travel a long way."

I nod, but I am not put off. "Yes, that is very nice, but can you get him off me now, please?"

The woman does not seem to register what I am saying to her. She smiles again, closes her eyes and puts her head back against the window.

Is she deaf? Does she not understand English? "Lady, please! This is my seat and that is yours! I paid for this seat and I would like to enjoy it, please." I push the kid towards her so she can see what I mean.

"Oh. OK. I am very sorry," she says, seeming to finally rouse herself. She shakes the boy gently and whispers, "Konani, wake up, boy. Wake up, Konani." But her whisper is barely a sound and her shaking only a pleasant rubbing that sends him deeper into sleep. I doubt she has any real intention of waking him up. She smiles that same toothless smile. "We is very tired and the child, he is very tired."

I feel saliva run down my arm, I am not impressed. "I do not care if he is a child or a dog, just get him off me!" At this point I am screaming. I am aware I am making a scene. I want the dripping child as far away from me as possible.

Everybody in the taxi looks back to see what the commotion is about. Another substantially-sized lady seated in front of me, who apparently heard the entire conversation, looks back at us and thinks it wise to add her unasked-for two cents. "*Haibo! Mare*, he's just a child. *Kganthe*, what kind of woman are you?" she says.

I cut a look at her, my eyes now frosted over: "The kind that doesn't want another woman's filthy child dirtying her work clothes with sweat and spit. But exactly how do you feature in this, mama?"

"*Mo lebale, mme. O ke satane*," the nosy fatty whispers, turning back around.

Yes, call me Satan, but next time mind your own bloody business, I think to myself. The woman next to me, clearly not very familiar with English but now finally understanding exactly what the problem is, struggles to lift her son back into her lap and, when this is unsuccessful, slaps the boy awake and yells at him for disturbing the poor lady. That's me. "I am very sorry, Sisi, we are very tired, we travel long way. Sorry," she says, placing the startled boy onto her lap. I nod and pull a tissue out of my handbag to dry my top.

"Thank you," I say, wiping my soggy sleeve. "That is all I asked for."

The taxi drops me off at the Schubert intersection, only a ten-minute walk away from Little Square Shopping

Centre. I have the option of asking the driver to do what they call 'a delivery' and drop me off inside Little Square but that will double my taxi fare, and although walking in the sun does nothing for my complexion, I need the money for my cosmetics and clothes. I see how the boys selling newspapers and cold drinks at the intersection look at me as I cross the street. "*Yo, o monthle ne,*" they say, "Hello, *nice,* need some help with those bags?" or "Let me walk you to work, *ngwana,*" or "Here, come have a drink, gorgeous, you look hot and tired." They whistle and holler and make fools of themselves trying to get my attention.

But I never look back. I adjust my posture (shoulders back and back upright), raise my chin and walk straight ahead without even the flutter of an eyelid. I walk right past them and their hot, flat cold drinks which I would never buy; right past their dusty newspapers all warm and grimy from dirty hands handling them all day, and past the revolting smell of the chicken feet which the peculiar, wrinkled old lady with charcoal-black skin and an odd orange umbrella sells at the corner.

I am not one of you, I want to tell them. Some day you will see me drive past here in a sleek air-conditioned car, and I will roll up my windows if you try to come near me, because *I am not one of you.* You are poor and black and I am rich and brown.

Working as a waitress is not very glamorous but I have to start somewhere. At least I am not packing plastics at Checkers or cleaning toilets. And Silver Spoon, I'll have you know, is no run-of-the-mill establishment. At Silver Spoon Coffee Shop I get to mix with the who's who of this country. Everybody from big-shot businessmen to surgeons and celebrated television producers. They all start their days at the Silver Spoon. Everybody knows us for our exotic coffee beans imported from Peru, El Salvador and New Guinea, for our peach and ginger iced teas made by Miss Becky herself, and our freshly baked cinnamon breads. Business deals are struck at Silver Spoon, deals that determine the strength of the rand and the price of gold. Alliances are formed at Silver Spoon and contracts signed for billions of dollars. In some of our quieter sections, actors and actresses practise their lines that are filmed and spoken on TV and heard by millions of South Africans every night on the evening soapies. Emails are sent from Silver Spoon Coffee Shop to Europe and back to Silver Spoon again.

Sometimes when we are not so busy I stand at the kitchen door and just observe the place and the people in it. I battle to take it all in. Sometimes while standing there at the kitchen door I am pulled out of my day-dreaming by a customer who wants my advice on an order or wants me to help them choose a colour for a fabric, and then I am reminded how essential I am to the functioning of Silver Spoon. They all know me. They call me Fiks.

"You try too hard."

141

"I beg your pardon?"

"You heard me. You try too hard, Fikile."

"Don't call me that here, Ayanda."

"Oh right. Fiks is it? Well Fiks, you try too hard."

"Thanks for that. I really do appreciate your views on how I should live my life, thank you very much indeed. But if you wouldn't mind I have a table waiting,"

"They don't care about you, Fikile."

"Who doesn't care about me?"

"Them, all those people out there."

"Really? Oh, well in that case, I am quitting right now! This instant! Immediately!"

"I'm being serious, Fikile. I've seen you out there. The way you fall over backwards for them. The way you run around like a headless chicken getting them this and that, stirring their tea anticlockwise and not clockwise as if they could even tell the difference."

"There is a difference."

"The effort you put into remembering even their middle names, their ridiculous little preferences, their favourite seats and those childish stories they tell about their lives and their dramas and their hardships.

It's real cute but are you aware that most of them don't remember you, even though they come here week after week? Do you know that if you were to walk past any one of them in the street on any other day of the week in some other place they wouldn't even know who you were? These people are not your friends, Fikile."

"I am not trying to make friends, Ayanda. I am just doing my job."

"Lies! You lie and lie and lie to yourself, Fikile, every day. How do you lie to yourself like that? Fikile?"

"Fuck, Ayanda, it's Fiks. Not Fikile, but Fiks. F-I-K-S, Fiks. Got it?"

I get to the restaurant five minutes early but when I arrive I have to check my watch again to make sure because Miss Becky's daughter, Carolina, is running frantically around the shop and so are the kitchen staff, who are already in plastic aprons and hair nets, their arms and faces covered in flour. I don't see Miss Becky or Ayanda anywhere.

"Why are you so late?" Carolina yells at me as she runs out of the shop carrying a wad of money in her hand.

I am not late, am I? It is Sunday, right? I look around for an answer. Yes it is Sunday, the Sunday papers are out on all the tables. The shop only opens at nine on a Sunday, and we arrive at eight. Right?

"Why are you still standing there?" Carolina shrieks as she runs back into the shop carrying a packet filled with bricks of butter. She screams more questions at me but gives me no opportunity to answer them.

I am not sure what it is I am supposed to do, so I follow her into the kitchen.

She throws the packet of butter onto the table already covered in eggshells and empty flour packets. "How many have you baked, Vincent?" she asks, stabbing a number on her phone.

"Only ten, ma'am," Vincent replies, looking up from the bread pans he is filling with dough, but making sure he does not make direct eye contact.

"Only ten!" she screeches. "Only ten?"

"Yes ma'am, only ten fit, ma'am, no space, ma'am, for –" Vincent is stammering. He is trying to explain that only ten loaves of bread fit into the oven at a time, but he is interrupted.

"Do you think this is a joke?" she squeals, her voice taking on an unnatural pitch. "Do you people think we are just teasing?" She looks around at all of us, daring us to respond. "There is no bread, people! No bread, none, zilch, so we have to make our own. Because you people think it is OK to go on strikes whenever it tickles your fancy, there is no bread today in any store. So we have to bake our own bread. There will be no hanging around, people. You are on your feet baking bread until we have enough loaves to stack them up to the ceiling. This place is opening up in an hour and we cannot serve customers if we have no bread.

"And you, sweetie," this she directs at me, "I don't want to see you standing around the shop looking around like an imbecile, as if you do not know you have work to do. Get on an apron and…" she waits for me to complete the sentence for her.

"Bake bread," I say, humiliated.

"Yes," she nods, "bake bread!"

I am mortified. I cannot believe I am being yelled at in this way in front of the kitchen staff. The bloody kitchen staff! Miss Becky would never degrade me in this manner. Miss Becky would never make me put on a plastic apron and a ridiculous hair net. It is her dumb daughter who has absolutely no understanding of how vital I am to the functioning of Silver Spoon, who has no appreciation for the hierarchy of Silver Spoon, that can go and disrespect me in that way in front of the kitchen staff. But I pull myself together.

"You heard her," I say to the kitchen staff after Carolina has left the room. "Stop standing around, and bake bread!"

They look at each other and then at me and shake their heads. "Shame," one of them mutters, as they get back to work.

Stupid people, I think, putting on an apron, why are they feeling sorry for me?

"I apologise. I never did introduce myself properly. My name is Fiks Twala. I have a second name, Fikile, which I never use because many find it too difficult to pronounce and, I must admit, I really do like Fiks better. I grew up in white environments for the most part of my life, from primary school right through to high school.

"Many people think I am foreign, from the UK or somewhere there. I think it is because my accent is so perfect and my manner so refined. Yes, I have always been different. I never could relate to other black South Africans. We've just never clicked. So I give them their space and they generally give me mine. It's never been an issue for me, though. I guess you do not miss something you have never known, so I do OK.

I lived in England for a while, Mummy and Daddy still lecture there. I couldn't stand the weather, absolutely dreadful, so I moved back here first chance I got. It's harder here, though, you have to do everything for yourself. You can't trust anybody, not with all the crime and corruption. But ja, it's home, what can I say?"

It wasn't all lies. I have never been able to relate to other blacks, that is the honest to God truth. Gogo with her endless praying, Uncle and his laziness, the dirty kids at school, I understood none of that. And the part about my name, well, I mean, everybody that matters to me calls me Fiks so it might as well be my first name. And what's the difference anyway? It's my name. Shouldn't I decide what I want to be called? I never had a father and Mama was a drunkard and a coward who ran out on life, leaving me alone, drenched in her wretched blood. So really, if anybody is allowed to create make-believe parents, it's me. Who does it hurt anyway? The pretend stories of my life serve the purpose they are required to fulfil, 'Fake it 'til you make it'. I feel no shame at my slight stretch of the truth.

"Well, look at you, Fiks, all geared up in apron and hair net, just like a good old housemaid," Miss Becky says laughing as she strolls into the kitchen, lollipop in hand and sunglasses in hair, oblivious to the hysteria in the room. She stops dead in her tracks when she becomes aware of the chaos around her. The kitchen is in shambles, there are eggshells on the floor, loaf tins scattered around, some greased and forgotten about, and a carton of milk, knocked onto its side, steadily dripping off the chopping counter.

Under Carolina's watch, nobody could get any one thing done without being screamed at for not already being onto the next thing, so as a result the kitchen went into panic mode. Miss Becky is furious. "Really now, people, can't I leave this place for one minute without it falling completely apart?"

Nobody says a word, not even Carolina. "Vincent? Yvonne? Happiness? What is going on back here? Tell me. Why must I always be here to baby you? Happiness, do this. Yvonne, do that. How many months have you been working here, Vincent? And still you cannot do a thing on your own." She does not shout, just speaks sternly and firmly in that calm Miss Becky manner that has a way of making one feel ashamed of oneself.

"And you, Fiks, dahling, exactly what are you doing in the kitchen? Customers will be arriving anytime soon and you are having a ball of a time back here." She doesn't wait for me to respond. "Please, clean yourself up and get out on the floor. You look disgusting. And the rest of you need to fix this place up. Yvonne, get things ready, orders will be coming in soon."

'A ball of a time'? Do I look as if I am having 'a ball of a time'? I am covered in flour; I have flour in my ears and flour in my eyes. Nobody in the kitchen was prepared to show me how to bake bread so I felt like an accomplished twit fumbling around with ingredients, trying to copy the others while Carolina kept coming in here sticking her big head in my face and screaming that I should bake bread or go home. How is any of that 'a ball of a time'?

"She really has been absolutely useless today," Carolina says to her mother, as she sits on the wash table, swinging her legs and sucking on a lollipop she fished out of her mother's bag as if she had absolutely nothing to do with the frenzy in the kitchen. "So did you manage to organise bread, Mom?"

Miss Becky stands with her hands on her hips, apparently still horrified at the state of the kitchen. "Well, yes, of course, Lina. Do you really think I would let some silly strike devastate the reputation of Silver Spoon? Never." And now, as if suddenly remembering a rage she'd felt earlier but had forgotten about, she turns on us. "And you listen well, people, what you do is really unacceptable. This business of striking must stop."

"I told them, Mom," Carolina butts in, but Miss Becky, now in full memory of what it was that upset her that morning, continues without any acknowledgement of Carolina's tittle-tattle. "Silver Spoon Coffee Shop has never disappointed its customers in all its years of existence and it is not about to, over some absurd bread strike. And you go tell that to your people when you get back home tonight. Striking is no way to solve any problems. It is selfish and completely inconsiderate and inconveniences millions of good people who depend on a daily supply of bread for their staple diets."

Of course I agree with her completely, but I know better than to interject now, so I let her continue.

"And this, dahlings, I say with the outmost sincerity: If any one of you here gets it into their heads to go marching up and down the streets thinking you can scare me with a strike, then you better be warned that I will have you replaced within hours, minutes." She clicks her gel-tipped, French painted nails. "Just like that."

The kitchen is silent. Nobody hazards a word.

"Well, get back to work, then." Miss Becky picks up her bag and turns to Carolina. "Come Lina, sit with me outside while I have my cigarette."

"Yes, Mom," Carolina says following her out, but not without having the final word: "I swear, Mom, I really do not know how you manage to work with these people."

"*Ma'am, the sandwich comes with cheese, that's why we call it a –*"

"*Well, I don't want it. Take it back.*"

"*Ma'am, if you give me your menu and allow me to read it for you, then you will see that –*"

"*Don't 'Ma'am' me, I can read, thank you very much. If it wasn't for us you wouldn't be able to read so don't you patronise me. Just take it back and bring me a cheese sandwich without dairy products, please!*"

"*I beg your pardon?*"

"*You people need to learn how to follow instructions.*"

"*'You people?'*"

"*Yes. You people need to learn how to follow instructions.*"

"Fuck you, Ma'am! Fuck you!"

I remember what a scene Ayanda made that day. Out of his frikkin' mind, swearing at a customer. I don't know why Ayanda works here. He comes from a wealthy family and does not need to be here. That's why he carries on like the people here owe him something. He was bloody lucky Miss Becky was not in the shop that day or else it would have been the end of his life at Silver Spoon, that's for sure. The boy totally lost it. He threw the women's cheese sandwich on the floor and then the plate and then his apron and then went marching into the kitchen.

"They feel no guilt, nothing! Did anybody hear that? 'If it wasn't for us you wouldn't be able to read.' Fuck her and her literacy: we'd be fucking better off without it, that's for damn sure. Fucking create our own means if they'd given us half the chance."

I had to do the damage control. I had to go out there and apologise for him. I had to make up some story about how he'd just had a loss in his life and was a little unstable. I had to calm the lady down because she was in tears. Poor woman had just found out she was lactose intolerant and was finding it difficult to deal with the news. She didn't need any of Ayanda's nonsense. The woman was actually very nice. If Ayanda hadn't been so obnoxious, maybe he would have found that out. The lady and I had a fat chat after I cleaned up the mess on the floor and brought her a glass of water. And so what if she was a little demanding at first, I would be too if I'd just found out I was lactose intolerant. It's pretty serious, life-changing news, you know. You have to always think about what you eat, try to figure out if there's milk in the food or not, otherwise it could kill you! Poor lady, I don't think she had anybody to speak to. And while she was pouring her heart out to me, Ayanda, of course, was tearing everything to shreds in the kitchen. He'd gone barking mad, talking all sort of revolution shit, scaring the poor kitchen staff.

"They feel nothing. They see nothing, absolutely nothing wrong with the great paradox in this country. Ten per cent of them still living on ninety per cent of the land, ninety per cent of us living on ten per cent of the land." Of course these statistics Ayanda was spitting out were completely outdated. That was then, this is now.

"Any fool with two neurons to rub together can see that there is a gross contradiction in this country." What was Ayanda talking about? He lived in some loft his parents had bought for him in Morningside.

"They do not see it because they do not care to see it. What good will it do them to think for us, to have a little consideration, just a little consideration for the fucking indigenous people of this fucking land you fuckers!"

Ayanda had completely lost his mind and was jeopardising the integrity of this establishment.

"They see no wrong in building their schools on our beloved soil, over our ancient trees, in the realms

of our sacred animals so that they can teach their children how to use us like parasites."

He wasn't even making any sense.

"How many of them do you hear saying that they want to leave the country? Huh? How many of them have you heard? Thousands, thousands of them want to leave. 'Oh the crime! Oh the poverty! No place to bring up a family.' So why don't they leave? Why the hell did they come here in the first place? We were doing just fine without them. If they want to leave, I say the sooner the better."

I knew he didn't mean that. He didn't mean any of it. Ayanda had tons of white friends, good friends, friends he cared about. Ayanda had gone to a white school, lived in white neighbourhoods all his life. He had the life that everybody dreamed of. The ass was just talking out of his arse. And we all knew it. I did, the kitchen staff did, and he did. So after that, he got back to work.

So the day has not started off as well as I would have liked, but so what? 'Failure isn't falling down, it is staying down', right? Isn't that how the saying goes? Well, I am no failure. I am all cleaned up now. I've touched up my make-up, fixed my hair and cleared my throat and am ready for my first table of the day.

"Good day, my name is Fiks. Is this your first time here? Well, welcome to Silver Spoon Coffee Shop.

153

I will be your waitress for today. I will be taking your orders and serving you your food. Here are our menus, there really is just so much to choose from so please do not hesitate to call me if you would like me to tell you a bit about the various dishes and some of the house favourites."

It's the thing you take for granted that turns out to be the most important thing in your life. I really believe that. Life is just shady like that. Like, I'm just thinking, now. Your accent, for example. It's not something most people give much thought to, let alone wish to change. But for me, my whole life has become about how I speak, about what sounds the words make as they fall on the listener's ear.

People don't realise how much their accent says about who they are, where they were born and most importantly what kind of people they associate with. Seriously, when we have those brief exchanges of words at the petrol station or in the bread queue, it is what you sound like that helps people to place you and determines how they'll treat you. Trust me, the accent matters. Don't let some fool convince you otherwise.

It is always exciting when we have virgins in the shop. We call them virgins, those people who come to Silver Spoon for the very first time. It is especially thrilling for me because each virgin represents a new opportunity, a shot at being discovered. I am always at my best when virgins come in. I want to give them the finest service and most sensational eating experience they have ever had in their lives. You never know who they may be, so that is why you never take chances. Some have been film producers shooting scenes in South Africa and we've even had a famous Australian actress on holiday here with her parents. But of course you only find out this stuff as they are about to leave, when they sign their bills or hand us their credit cards. By then it is too late, the impression has been made and, if it's bad, you have lost out on a potentially grand opportunity. So I never take chances. Always the best service, me at my best, always as if I am serving the Queen of England.

The family of virgins I have now do not look very spectacular or very rich. Actually more bland and Orange Farm-ish, than rich and famous. When I brought them their food, they held hands and prayed. Rich people don't pray. But you never know with these celebrity families. They may just be doing that to throw us off.

I do not pray. Gogo did enough praying to cover me and all my descendants from here to Kingdom Come. It was strange because she wasn't terribly religious during the day, in fact she was pretty unscrupulous in the way she lived her life, and Uncle, who was very religious during the day but not so holy at night, would tell me not to listen to a word Gogo said because her way of life would secure me the presidential suite in hell. I wasn't too sure about that, because the way Gogo prayed at night, dragging me out of bed and making me kneel down beside her, the candle in my hand burning hot wax into my skin, well, I didn't think any god I'd ever heard of would deny such desperate prayer even just a mattress in heaven.

"Father, I do not doubt that you love your children,"
she would say.

"I do not doubt that you love all your children."
Stressing the 'all'.

"I do not doubt that you made us all as equals, I do
not doubt that when you created this earthly home,
that all within was for us all to share."

"I do not doubt, Lord, that some day it will be as you
intended." And then she would begin to sob.

"But which day, Lord? On which day will it be as you
desired?"

Gogo must have whined that same prayer every night of
the school holidays I spent with her in Hammanskraal,
and she probably whined it just as often when I wasn't
there. I didn't get the point. Surely you ask God for
something once, twice, maybe even three times, but
when you still don't get what you want, then maybe,
just maybe, it's safe to conclude that God's answer is
'No, Gogo'. You don't just keep nagging and nagging
for the same thing every night for the rest of your life.
There's just no sense in that. You simply accept your
lot and move on. Poor God, having to listen to Gogo
beg and beg night after night must have been agony.
God must be glad she is now dead so that He can
tell it to her face: "No, Gogo!" But knowing Gogo,
she's probably there in heaven, still nagging Him and
nagging Him, hoping He'll change His mind.

Maybe things were never intended to be equal. That was Gogo's first mistake. She just assumed that God intended things to be equal amongst all his children. That is why she lived her life in gloom, always hoping that tomorrow God would find the time or check His diary and remember, 'Oh yes, got to sort out the inequalities on earth', and zap his wand and fix everything. Gogo, she never considered that perhaps God made some races superior, as an example for other races to follow. If only someone had suggested that theory to Gogo, then she would have spared herself (and me!) a whole lot of carpet burn and time spent sending off bootless prayers.

Shame. It wasn't all bad. In fact on some holidays the evenings spent praying would actually be quite a bit of fun. During those holidays Gogo would be restless and impatient and we would not bother with the candles or kneeling. Instead we would march around the house, Gogo leading and me repeating after her. It was especially fun when Gogo heard news of young black boys going missing in the cities, or news of another one of her maid friends being raped by the baas of the family they worked for. Then Gogo would grow so mad she'd stomp and yell and shout right at God, right into His face, so loud that I was afraid God might come down any minute and strike her down with His mighty hand and yell in Grandpa's voice (who was at that stage long dead), "O a nthasetsa, ke bogetse bolo!"

"How long, Lord?" she would scream, drunk on emotion.

157

"How long, Lord?" I would scream too, excited at the performance that was to begin.

"No longer can we wait."

"No longer can we wait," I would agree.

"For I fear, Father."

"For I fear, Father."

"I fear for the patience of your children."

"I fear for the patience of your children."

"They grow restless, Lord." Her voice would be trembling now.

"They grow restless, Lord." I'd try make my voice tremble, too.

"They tire of waiting."

"They tire of waiting."

"I do not doubt you, Lord!" Here Gogo would throw her body to the ground.

"I do not doubt you, Lord!" And my body would follow.

"You, Father, are mighty and great."

"You, Father, are mighty and great."

"But Father..." and her voice would tremble again.

"But Father..." mine would as well.

"I cannot say with such certainty the same for myself."

"I cannot say with such certainty the same for myself."

"No, Lord, I cannot be sure."

"No, Lord, I cannot be sure."

At this point, Gogo, now exhausted from her demonstration, would just lie there on the floor sobbing softly. I did not know how to sob like her so I would just lie at her feet, repeating after her and trying to sound as sad as possible.

"I do not know, Father..."

"I do not know, Father..."

"...where this new self may take me."

"...where this new self may take me."

"Suddenly I am filled with a rage that delights me."

"Suddenly I am filled with a rage that delights me."

159

"I do not know how much more I can swallow."

"I do not know how much more I can swallow."

"In my dreams I spit vengeance."

"In my dreams I spit vengeance."

"Oh no Lord, it is not you I doubt..."

"Oh no Lord, it is not you I doubt..."

"...but me."

"...but me."

It's the virgins at the table by the fan, and next to them the Potgieters, who love their steaks all soft and bloody and prefer to sit as far away from the smoking section as possible because Nerissa, their youngest daughter, is asthmatic. *Mrs Potgieter is expected to give birth March third so remember to ask about the baby.* Then comes in Mr Wilkinson and his daughters Tammy *(berry smoothie without the lumpy stuff)* and Monica, who is going to grade one next year. Next is Pamela, with her crocodile skin purse lined with credit cards, whom I seat near the Wilkinsons because I know she has a thing for Mr Wilkinson and loves the way he loves his little girls. After Pamela is Megan *(Savanna without ice, change ashtray frequently)* and Sheila *(peach and apple tea and choc-bit waffle with cream, man-trouble so sympathise).* At around 10.30 a large group of virgins walk in who don't look like they are going to eat much, so I seat them outside in the sun so that they do not stay long. The virgins are followed by James. I've saved him the table by the window with the view of the gym swimming pool downstairs. He's a disgusting pervert but tips me well, so I grant him his little indulgences. And then some more virgins.

These are my kind of people. People with stuff to show for themselves. Lots of stuff! Ja, they all have their bad sides, like all people do, but they do not let that get in the way of them making something of themselves. I can really relate to these people, that is why I am so good at this job. We have so much in common, so much to talk about. I understand them. They understand me. Not like the people at home whose minds are still lodged in the past.

"The virgins at the table near the cakestand, dahling, have been waiting for their order for about ten minutes now." Miss Becky says this while walking up to me with that smile on her face that you know is not for you but for the customers, who may grow uneasy if they see how angry she is.

My stomach sinks. I forgot about them. Shoot. It's just so busy today, and with Sarah and Dave sending me back and forth because they can't make up their minds about what they want to eat (as usual) and little Monica repeatedly throwing spoons onto the floor and Mr Wilkinson insisting I keep bringing her new ones, well, I am kind of battling to keep up with it all. But I'm not complaining, I love Sarah and Dave and Mr Wilkinson's girls, and I guess they're allowed to throw stuff around? It's just a bad day. Shit. I can't believe I forgot to place that order, virgins for that matter; guess I can forget about getting their tip.

"Where is Ayanda, Miss Becky?" I tentatively ask her, as I punch the virgins' order into the machine.

"Don't 'where is Ayanda' me, Fiks. You should be able to run this place by yourself without Ayanda. You've been here long enough. Watch your tone with me, madam."

What tone?

"Now go. Go push their order up in the kitchen while I calm them down."

What tone? What was my tone? I really need to pull it together. I need to watch what I say. I cannot afford to upset Miss Becky. I cannot afford to forget to place orders. Where is Ayanda? What is wrong with me today? Fiks, stop 'where is Ayanda-ing' and focus on work. Work, work, work. Focus, focus, focus. Sort out the virgins order, get cigarettes for Chantelle (*Peter Stuyvesant, Extra Mild*), offer Emily's parents the dessert menu and find more sweets for baby Kim.

"Add two more cups of flour, Fikile."

"But why?"

"Because we need to make another batch, Fikile."

"*I don't want to do this anymore, Gogo.*"

"*Fikile, just add two more cups of flour, please dear, you can see my hands are full.*"

"*But how come you never bake for me, Gogo?*"

"*Stop with that, Fikile.*"

"*How come you never make cupcakes for me, Gogo?*"

"*I don't have money, Fikile.*"

"*But you have money to bake for madam's children!*"

"*It's madam's money, Fikile. Now stir that please, and don't spill.*"

"*I don't want to do this anymore.*"

"*Fikile, I am not asking you, I am telling you. Stir please, the children will be back now. So stop with your nonsense and stir. We still need to walk the dogs.*"

"*But you hate dogs, Gogo, they give you sinuses.*"

"*Yes, Fikile, but Gogo needs money to eat, so Gogo must walk the dogs.*"

"*But I don't like those dogs, Gogo. They scare me. I don't want to walk the dogs.*"

163

"*I cannot leave you in this house alone, Fikile. Madam will not be happy. You will just have to be brave. Now get those cherries out of the fridge for Gogo.*"

"*I'll walk the dogs for you if you give me a cupcake, Gogo, then you won't have to worry about your sinuses being blocked tonight.*"

"*Stop it, Fikile.*"

"*Please Gogo, just one cupcake, just one, nobody will even notice.*"

"*I'm sorry, my darly, on your birthday, nê? Gogo will bake for you on your birthday.*"

"*You always say that, Gogo, you always say that but you never do. You love madam's children more than you love me!*"

"*I shouldn't have brought you here, Fikile, you're just a nuisance.*"

"Fiks, dahling! Won't you show the gentleman and his lovely wife and daughter to their table, please?" Miss Becky startles me out of my thoughts. I turn around and want to scream out in agony when I see who it is.

Them. The Tlous. The family that I hate with everything in me. Where is Ayanda? This is his family, he knows I do not serve the black families, they're just an annoyance and waste of my time. Especially this specific family. I hate them. I hate them so much.

I don't know why they come here. Every Sunday they come, nobody knows who they are, they do not fit in here, everybody can see it, everybody knows it, I am sure they know it too, but they come anyway. Such forced individuals. New money is what they are and that is why I hate them. That is why I avoid them. Where is Ayanda when you need him? The bastard. He doesn't mind them; he actually enjoys waiting on them. It makes him feel better, like he's reaching out to his own or whatever. But I don't care about any of that crap, I just want them to leave.

"Fiks!" Miss Becky yells, pushing them towards me, clearly uncomfortable with the family she knows she should probably be acquainted with better because they are here every Sunday. I groan, wondering if this day can get any worse.

At first it seems as if there is no table for them. I am relieved. Maybe they will leave and go some place else. But Miss Becky, always the one to find a solution, pulls up the table that we use to keep the kitchen door open and organises three chairs. She gives me her signal and I show them where to sit. The mother, hair and nails all done up, looks at me as she sits and smiles. I do not smile back. I know her smile is fake. I know when they look at me with those pitying eyes they are all really laughing at me inside. "Did you see her?" they will whisper as I turn my back. "Those cheap clothes and those old shoes! Poor thing, we really should give her our leftovers." I know what they are like, these BEE families. Fake hearts and fake lives all dressed up in designer labels bought yesterday. I place their menus on the table and walk away without a word. I have real customers to serve.

"Melissa, here is your decaf Moccachino. Now tell me, how was London?"

"When did you get back, Mike? It's so great to see you again! We've missed you and your madness!"

"George, this espresso is on me. You look like death. I'm guessing we had a big night last night?"

"I know exactly what you need, Peter, something real greasy coming up!"

"Oh really Mr Potgieter, you don't need to do that, I'm only doing my job. Thank you, Mr Potgieter, I do appreciate it. See you next Sunday."

"Another waffle, Sheila? I know, I hate men too! I'm so sorry, Sheilz, but you'll see, everything will be OK. It's his loss, not yours."

"Come, give Aunty Fiks a hug before you leave! Look what I found for you, my angels; lollipops! Now be good, don't give your Daddy too much trouble. Bye, guys, see you next Sunday!"

It may have been all those magazines that I started reading. I had spent my whole holiday at Gogo's indoors and reading one magazine after another. Body, Catalogue Girl, Gloss, Fly Girl, Allure, Panache, Spoilt!, Chic, Live Life. Gogo collected them from the white homes she worked at. The wives and daughters often threw them out before they even finished them. The more magazines I read, the more I wanted to read, and soon Uncle's dusty old novels were out of the window and magazines were my bedside reading, my can't-sleep-at-night reading, my afternoon tea reading, my only reading. I lived in those magazines, and the more I read, the more assured I was that the life in those pages was the one I was born to live. From who supermodel Christine Pau was dating to what perfume Gabrielle was wearing to the Grammys, I knew it all. At the age of fifteen I could even advise you what to pack when spending a weekend away in the Bahamas.

So when I got back to school in January, Vula Mehlo Secondary School, mind all air-brushed and sweetly scented in Ridgley's new fragrance, I felt strangely out of place, detached, as if I was watching them. Bo Zanele, bo Thabo, bo Meshoe seemed to be on Bop TV in black and white. They were so dull, so dirty, smelling of petroleum jelly and wearing the same old faded brown tunics, white socks (now yellow) and worn school shoes. Their hair was done, plaited neatly into rows for the new year, but I knew, come next month, it would be filled with sand and itching because it hadn't been washed in weeks. Everything they said and worried about bored me.

I did not care anymore whether I thought Shoki's parents might make her marry Simba because he made her pregnant. I didn't care about the guys at the car wash who would buy us air time if we let them see our stuff. It was only a month, a month of litchi, lime and mint cocktails in the pages of those magazines, but a month enough. It was like I was a puzzle-piece, pulled out of the puzzle and bent and now I could never fit back in. I'd seen pictures of another life, a better life, and I wanted it. So I walked out of the school gates and never went back. That was 1999, the beginning of grade ten, the beginning of Project Infinity.

"Casey, dear, do you want me to refill that? No, sweetheart, it's my pleasure."

"Your first time at Silver Spoon sir? Well, welcome. You are going to be a regular, I can just tell."

"Josh! You are such a flirt! Does your wife know about you?"

"Timothy, your Mommy is right, you must eat your veggies. I promise to let you have a taste of all our ice creams if you do."

"So, how's the new boyfriend? Tell me all, I can see you are bursting to."

"Oh, I'm sorry, did I not introduce myself properly? My name is Fiks, Fiks Twala. I have a second name, Fikile, which I never use…"

I think even before I consciously decided it, I already knew that this was the kind of life I was meant to live. The Silver Spoon life. The holidays abroad, the cashmere, the dramas at Mixy on a Friday night, the smashed R1.2 million cars, the tears over a bad break-up and the retail therapy after. The more time I spent with these people, listening to their stories, peeking in on their day-to-days, the more certain I was that the lives they lived were a reflection of the life I was born to live. I never did have the stomach for poverty. I am too sensitive. I could never deal with all that trash.

Paul walks into the shop, still in his suit, the same suit since Friday. He's with two other men, both very drunk. James finally leaves after another Sunday morning spent watching women climb into and out of the gym pool. I seat them at his table, Paul with his back against the window and the other two at his sides. I do not want him distracted.

"Hi, Fiks."

"Hi, Paul."

"No kiss today?"

"I'm working, Paul!"

"You done something new to your hair?"

"No, Paul."

"Well, it looks good. You look good, as always."

"Thank you, Paul."

Paul has been in here every day this week. Virgin on Monday and regular ever since. I know he wants me, that is the only reason he keeps coming here. He never eats, just buys a drink or two and then pays with a R200 bill and tells me to keep the change.

But I'm no whore, I made that clear to him when he came in for the first time on Monday, flashing his money around and calling me 'baby.' He left a couple of hundred rands and his phone number and got up and left. I ran out after him. "Sorry sir," I said, "you seem to have left some of your belongings behind." 'Belongings'? Ja, I know, it sounded smarter in my head.

He laughed and then said, "Those belongings are yours, sweetheart."

"I'm afraid we are not allowed to accept such extravagant gifts from customers, sir, it gives them the wrong ideas," I told him.

"What kind of ideas?" he asked.

"The wrong kind."

That's when he grabbed my arms and pulled me towards him. "Would this be wrong?" he asked and then kissed me before I had a chance to figure out what was going on.

That was Monday, almost exactly a week ago, and today we were flirting as if we were old friends who had been estranged before the friendship had an opportunity to blossom, meeting once again after many years. Perhaps we really were old friends, friends from a previous lifetime. Maybe that is the explanation of the instant connection between us. I have had older white men look at me before, but not like Paul. The other men were just bored and horny but Paul, Paul is different.

Infinity.

Mrs Zodwa had said it was a number larger than any number that could be imagined.

How crazy, I had thought. "Then it is no number at all," I had yelled out.

It's a concept, Mrs Zodwa had explained, expressed by the symbol ∞.

I got up from my desk and looked it up in the dictionary on the bookshelf. I did not believe that such a thing existed. Of course I was only eleven then, unable to comprehend something so endless and so boundless.

Infinity. It came to represent all I strove for in life. It became my secret word, a charm I hung around the neck of my soul, the key to something limitless. I knew that some day I would achieve Project Infinity. It did not matter that I was not exactly sure what Project Infinity was, because I knew it would be infinitely better than where I was then. I would leave this life of blackness and embark on something larger than large and greater than great, something immeasurable and everlasting.

"Fiks, dahling, the Tlous? Have you taken the Tlous' orders yet?" Miss Becky says, looking a little flustered. She holds a broken plate in her hand and her cheeks are red, hinting that she is slightly stressed.

"The who?"

"The Tlous. They are still sitting with their menus. What has gotten into you today, sweetheart? Goodness me. I really do hope the taxi strikes come to an end soon, I need Ayanda here, you're useless on your own."

What? I can't believe this. She thinks Ayanda isn't at work because the taxis are striking? Such bullshit! Ayanda doesn't even take a taxi to work, his father drops him off in his shiny Chrysler at the Schubert intersection every morning.

"He's lying," I say to Miss Becky, regretting it immediately.

"Who's lying?"

"Ayanda, about the taxi strikes. He's lying."

"It's in the paper, Fiks, on the radio. There's strikes everywhere, Fiks, everybody knows that." She shakes her head and is about to walk away, but then stops, looks at me for a while, as if she is seeing me for the very first time, and then speaks. "You shouldn't be so vindictive, Fiks, it's not good for the spirit. Ayanda is my favourite because he works hard." She pauses again. "So work hard."

"Yes, Miss Becky," I say, wishing I had just left the whole thing alone. But I am right! Yes, there are strikes going on but they are the bread company strikes, not taxi strikes. Why is it that I am always the one in the wrong? Ayanda's the favourite yet he's sitting on his arse at home in his family's mansion while I'm here breaking my back.

"You are still standing here?" Miss Becky is screaming now. "The Tlous, Fiks! The Tlous!" Miss Becky never screams.

I hurry over to their table. They are all still there. I thought if I'd wished them away, I'd turn around and they'd be gone. Oh no, not them, they're not going anywhere, they are bent on making my day hell. The daughter agitatedly moves her cell phone from hand to hand. When I get to their table she looks at me with such deep disdain I want to rip those snotty 'I am better than you' eyeballs out their sockets and crush them under my foot.

"Hi. My name is Fiks. Are you ready to order?"

"Yes, we have been for some time now," the daughter says, irritated, her ugly face all scrunched up in a scowl, her large nose up in the air.

"I apologise. We've been very busy today," I manage to get out, not prepared to let her make me lose my cool.

"Yes, we've noticed that *you've* been very busy indeed." She says this with a smirk, her eyes pointing

173

to Paul's table, who sits there staring at me. He sees us looking at him and blows me a kiss.

"What's that supposed to mean?" I snap back. She does not respond, but instead carries on fidgeting with her cell phone.

"Ofilwe, don't be so rude to the nice, pretty girl," the father says, as if suddenly realising the tension around him. "Three Traditional English Breakfasts please, sweetie, and some orange juice." He winks at me. The mother fires a warning look at him.

Screw it, I think. And wink back before walking away.

I can smell new money from a mile away. I do not need any background information. You do not need to even open your mouth. Just a two-second head-to-toe analysis and I am able to identify you as the real thing or that other thing. I am very seldom wrong. I give you ten minutes at most, and you will have exposed yourself. When I ask you if you want your pasta with penne, fettuccine or spaghetti, you will ask me which is the biggest. If I ask you if you want feta cheese in your salad, you will say, 'Yes, grated please'. When I go get your fruit smoothie, you will stop me and say, thinking that you are really smart, 'Make it decaf!'

Why am I so good at this, at picking you fakers out? Because I cannot stand people like you. You sicken me. You remind me of everything I do not want to be.

That is why I need to be able to identify you as early as possible. So I can avoid you at all costs.

Paul calls me over to their table. "We're leaving now," he says when I get there.

"OK, so I'll go get your bill then." I respond, a little disappointed. I was hoping he'd stay longer, play for a little longer, maybe even take me home so I don't have to ride back in that wretched train.

"Sure. You coming with?" he asks, reaching for my hand. I pull away. Miss Becky would fire me on the spot if she saw me holding hands with a customer.

His friends start to laugh. "Your wife know you so feverish, Paul?" one of them asks.

The other looks at me and smiles. "Jungle fever, honey. Jungle fever. You know what that means?"

"Ignore them, Fiks," Paul cuts in. "Come with me. How much are they paying you here? I'll give you what you make here in a year, today. I'll even double it. Triple it. You don't belong here."

Paul's not lying. He probably could give me what I make at Silver Spoon in a single day. Paul reeks of money. But I am not for sale, am I?

His phone rings. Paul looks at the screen and quickly switches it off. He places a couple of hundred on the table. "Will this cover the bill, Fiks?"

I nod. The three of them get up. They struggle a bit, using their chairs and the table to help them up, not because they're drunk but because they are so old. For the first time I wonder how old Paul really is. Sixty, maybe even seventy.

"Think about it, Beautiful," he whispers, as they leave the shop. "I'll be back for you."

I do not know in which form Project Infinity will present itself to me, but I do not think it will be obvious. That is why I do not let a single opportunity slip me by without giving it some serious consideration. Like this waitressing job at Silver Spoon. It isn't exactly spectacular living but it is a stepping stone which allows me to mingle with the A-list, who will some day be friends and neighbours. People like me have to make difficult choices. We were not the fortunate ones who were born into the lap of luxury, and so we have to fight our way there. Anything worth having in life comes at a price, a price that is not always easy to pay. Maybe Paul is right. Maybe it is time I leave Silver Spoon. And so what if the world does not approve of us? He seems to really like me and I enjoy his company. What do I have to lose?

The Tlous eventually leave. Of course they go without leaving a tip, but then again, what more does one expect from black people? The shop begins to quieten down as the brunch crowd leaves. I get out the broom and sweep the floor. After this I will wipe the tables down and push the chairs in. I hope Miss Becky sees me taking some initiative.

I hate this time of day, when the shop is still and there are few people to socialise with. When things are still, time seems to drag on and soon you have done all there is to do and are left with nothing so you are forced to think. And that is exactly when your mind thinks it a handsome idea to deliberate over all that deep and meaningful stuff, which quite frankly gives me a headache. I am not shallow, I just have too many of my own problems to try to solve the rest of the world's. I really just can't be involved.

I need to spring-clean my head. There is a real big mess up there but I am too afraid to go in because I do not think I have the strength to handle the task of tidying it all. It is a long time since I was there last. I am scared of what I may find. I am fearful of the cluttered floor, the dusty shelves, the locked cases, the stuffed drawers, the broken bulbs and the cracked windows.

Two young guys walk into the shop. They do not wait to be seated but head straight for one of the tables inside. One of them gets up and grabs an ashtray from the pile I have stacked on a tray and left on one of the side tables to clean up later. He empties it onto the floor, sits back down at the table, and lights a cigarette.

"Welcome to Silver Spoon Coffee Shop, gentlemen, would you like me to show you to the smoking section outside?" I ignore the ash on the floor I have just swept clean.

"We are fine here thanks, Peach," the one with the cigarette says without looking at me.

"I am afraid it is shop policy, sir, that if you wish to smoke, you have to sit in the smoking section. There's a very nice table I can show you –"

"We're fine, really, thanks, hun. Mind getting us some menus?" He takes another puff of his cigarette and blows rings into the air. His friend looks at me and shrugs. I sigh and go get them their menus.

There are no other people in the shop now so I guess it is OK, I tell myself. But as soon as a non-smoking customer walks in they are going to have to move outside, with no negotiations! I sweep the ash from the floor, and pick up the stack of ashtrays so I can take them to the back. But before I can get through the door I see Miss Becky walking into the shop. She spots the two guys at the table, walks over to them to give her usual Silver Spoon welcome, and before I can rush in to explain, she sees the cigarette and throws a cold look up at me standing helplessly at the storeroom door with a pile of ashtrays in my hands. She tells them she hopes they enjoy their meal and marches up to me.

"So you want to explain to me, dahling, why the gentleman is sitting with a cigarette in the non-smoking section of the shop? Are you trying to get this shop closed down?"

"He wouldn't move, Miss Becky."

"He wouldn't move? Why didn't you ask them whether they wanted to be in the smoking section before you seated them, Fiks?"

"They seated themselves, Miss Becky."

"They seated themselves? Oh, Fiks! You allowed customers to seat themselves?" She shakes her head, and raises her hand to stop me as I attempt to explain. "You really are intent on working on my nerves today, aren't you, dahling?"

I try to speak again, but am once again stopped by her hand. She takes a deep breath, in and out, and then coolly walks over to the table with the two guys. She smiles her large Miss Becky smile, puts her hand on the one with the cigarette's shoulder, says something that makes them laugh and then nod and then laugh again and then get up and move outside. Miss Becky calmly walks back to me. "The young gentlemen had no problem with sitting in the smoking section, dahling. If only you had taken the time to explain to them that the inside of the shop is for non-smokers only, then we wouldn't have to be having this conversation."

"But I did –"

"I do not want to hear it, Fiks. I think I've had enough of you for one day." She closes her eyes, breathes deeply again, and then says, "Maybe you should just go home."

"Go home? But Miss Becky it's only –"

"Yes Fiks, go home and think about your behaviour. I'll get Yvonne to take over from you. We'll speak again on Monday." She does not wait for me to say anything, but takes the ashtrays out of my hands and walks into the storeroom calling for Yvonne.

Go home? But it's only two o'clock. How can Miss Becky be sending me home at two o'clock? There are another three whole hours before the shop closes and I am being sent home? What about the customers? They won't be happy if Fiks is not here. They need me. Yvonne has no waitressing experience. Yvonne can barely speak English, she won't ever manage. This thing I do, this waitressing thing at this shop, takes a certain kind of person. A person with people skills, a person who knows how to speak to the rich and famous without making them feel uncomfortable. This job requires a person who has an understanding of the Silver Spoon world and the kind of people who live in it. A person like me. Yvonne understands none of that.

My cheeks dampen. One day Miss Becky will see that this place is nothing without me. She'll be so sorry she sent me home early that when I come in tomorrow morning she'll be down on her knees begging me to forgive her. But I won't, I'll tell her that I am leaving with Paul and taking my style, my talent and my manner with people with me, and never coming back.

Sometimes I feel it all collapsing around me. My face gets so hot that I cannot even breathe.

I am suddenly aware of the boy outside watching me. It's the friend, the one who was not smoking, the one who shrugged his shoulders. I am embarrassed as I realise that he has been watching me this whole time, watching while Miss Becky scolded me, watching as I wet my cheeks. He smiles when he sees that I can see him. "I am sorry," he mouths through the glass. I look away, and go to the back to get my stuff. Whatever.

I am tired of waiting, waiting for the day when it will all be different, when it will be my turn, my story, my rose.

I am tired of the fear, the anxiety, the endless debates within my head, the empty feeling in my chest and the knot in my stomach.

I am tired of looking around, in the mirror, at my legs and my hands, wondering when they will be different.

I am tired of the same outfit worn in different styles. I am tired of sleepless nights, phone calls to far-away places, crossed fingers and bended knees.

I am tired. I have tried, I am always trying, but now I am tired. I want it now.

Yvonne waves as I walk out of the shop, yanking her hair net and plastic apron off and tucking in the Silver Spoon T-shirt Miss Becky has lent her. It is evident that she is insanely excited. She waves at me but I do not wave back. There is only one Fiks, and nobody else can do what I do.

The boy, the friend, the one who was not smoking, the one who shrugged his shoulders, the one who smiled, the one who mouthed "I am sorry," gets up from his chair and runs after me.

I do not stop and hear the other guy, the one who emptied the ashtray onto the floor after I had just swept it, the one who lit a cigarette in the non-smoking section, the one who lied to Miss Becky about what happened, shout, "What is it with you and black girls, Sky! It's fucking embarrassing, dude! Leave the chick alone, man!"

I walk faster. Those words make my eyes fill again. I want him to leave me alone but he catches up to me.

"Sheesh," he gasps, out of breath. "I'm not trying to mug you, lady, I just wanted to apologise for what happened there earlier."

Before I can help it my cheeks are drenched.

"I hope we didn't get you fired or anything. My friend has issues, don't let him get to you. I don't actually know why I'm friends with him. He's a real jerk. I can speak to your boss-lady if you want, I really don't want you to lose your job because of us. I really am sorry."

I nod, but cannot get any words out.

"I am *so* sorry. This job obviously means a lot to you. I am really sorry. Please don't cry. I'll go speak to your boss. Do you want me to speak to her?"

I shake my head. Gosh no, I think, that's the last thing I need. He does that and she'll send me home for good. "No," I manage to say, drying my eyes with a bunch of Silver Spoon napkins I keep in my bag. "It's fine, I'm fine."

Even if I cry all night, I am fine.
Even though my heart is punctured, I am fine.
Even though I feel like there is no hope, I am fine.
Even though it feels like it will be this way forever, I am fine.
Even though it makes no sense, I am fine.

"I really do hate to see such a beautiful girl so sad," he says, smiling, relieved that I have stopped crying. "*Kumuhle kakhulu.*" He says this with a confidence that makes me think that this guy has used this line before. But I cannot help laughing at his silliness. I wonder if he is saying it wrong intentionally

"*Umuhle,*" I say, correcting him anyway.

"Thank you," he smiles, thinking I am returning the compliment. I realise that it was a sincere mistake and not just a white boy's silliness. How sweet, I think. How refreshing.

"No, it's *Umuhle,* not *Kumuhle.*" I explain.

"Oh," he laughs. "Well, *Umuhle*."

Such a nice boy, I think.

If it was another day and I was not being sent home and replaced by a kitchen maid, I might have been disappointed that the moment was spoilt by the friend's rude interruption. "Sky, I didn't come here to watch you run after every black chick that walks past."

I look at my watch and realise that if I want to catch the 3.30 train I need to leave and find a taxi now. "Thank you," I say, and walk away.

"The name is Sky, Sky Richardson," he shouts to my back as I move further and further away. "We should have coffee some time, a drink or whatever. I'll come find you. Hey, you didn't tell me your name!" he yells, but I don't stop and keep walking until I can't hear him anymore.

Sky. Such a nice name.

There's a couple of taxis standing empty on the corner of Schubert when I get there. So much for the taxi strikes, Miss Becky.

We wait for forty minutes until the taxi fills up and we finally leave. It is Sunday, and everybody is tired, lost in his or her own thoughts, wondering where the weekend went, so the drive back to the station is quiet. I remind the driver to stop at the station so I can get out. It is 3.50 when I get to the platform where I board the train for Mphe Batho, so because I am twenty minutes late, I have to wait for the 4.30 train. The station is empty and there are numerous benches to choose from. I am a little uneasy being here alone, so decide against reading my magazine and instead sit on my bag and keep my eyes wide open and watchful for any strange activities.

When the train arrives at 5pm and not 4.30 as is timetabled, I am surprised to see the gentleman I was on the train with this morning sitting in the same place. Before I can pretend to have not seen him, he waves and beckons me to come sit next to him and a little girl he seats on his lap to make room for me.

"You have a daughter?" I ask as I sit down.

"Yes, her name is Palesa." He says proudly. "*Yithi molo ngo sisi Palesa*, say hello to the nice lady, Palesa."

The 'nice lady'? I silently chuckle. That's a first! I never thought anybody around here would refer to me as 'the nice lady'. Such a strange man, I think to myself. How can he call me the 'nice lady' after the way I treated him this morning? The little girl looks at me and smiles. She is pretty. He picks her up and places her on the seat opposite to him.

"Yes, she was with her grandmother for the weekend. We are going home now, nê Paly?" he says, sticking his tongue out at her. She giggles.

"She did not want to come home, her granny spoils her so much," he continues, laughing.

I'm not sure why this man is being so nice to me. Has he forgotten our earlier encounter? The apple that rolled out of the empty briefcase? Perhaps it is not the same man. I look at his feet for the briefcase to make sure. *Mr K.J. Fishwick*. No, it's him alright.

He catches me looking at it and laughs again. "You really do like this briefcase, don't you?"

I smile, embarrassed. "It is nice" is all I can get out.

"You think? I find it to be such a nuisance. I only carry it around to make my boss feel better. He made such a big deal of giving it to me. It was my birthday last week and when he heard he pulled all his papers and cards and pens and things out of the briefcase and gave it to me right there and then. Everybody at the office made such a fuss about the whole thing, you'd think he'd bought me a house or something. But I really have no need for it. I never have anything to put in it, except apples of course, that is, when they don't roll away." He laughs again. His laugh is contagious and I catch myself laughing with him. I am ashamed, too. I know I must apologise but do not know how. I search for a long time for the words but all I can think to say is, "Maybe your boss made such a fuss because the briefcase is so expensive."

"It is?" he asks.

"Yes, it is a V&CX briefcase. That's a very expensive label."

"Oh," he says nodding, but is not moved by the revelation as one might have expected.

We sit in silence. I look out the window and realise that next stop we will be home.

Sunday afternoons are always pretty quiet on the train and I am often back home in no time. But for some reason, today I do not want the train to stop.

"I went to pick up Palesa from school on Friday…"

Despite myself, I turn around and face him, like people do when they speak to each other. He is a very handsome man, handsome and kind.

"Oh, really?" I say, encouraging him to go on.

"So while I am waiting for her to find her schoolbag and say goodbye to her friends, my eyes start to wander around the playground. I stand there, listening to what sounds like millions of laughing, screaming, smiling little faces filled with so much life and energy. Most of them were milky white, but here and there were spots of colour." He stops. I do not know if that is the end of his story, so I wait.

"They seemed so happy, you know, and their happiness so pure and real you could grab it in your two hands." I am not sure where this is going, but I remain silent.

"I asked one of the teachers to show me where the bathroom was. After a long day at work I was feeling a little overwhelmed by the heat and all the buzzing around me. It was Friday, so that meant that they, the little kids, weren't going to come to school for a whole two days, so their excitement was understandable." He chuckles that goofy chuckle again and this time I laugh with him, without inhibition. I have no idea what he is speaking about but for some reason it's just so good to listen to him speak.

"And then suddenly a little chocolate girl walks past me, hand in hand with the cutest half-metre milk bar I have ever seen in my life. Both of them are chatting away, both with fizz-pops in their other hands." He smiles at the memory. "Wow! I thought, look how happy they are. Who am I to get in the way?"

Now I am completely lost. "What do you mean?" I hesitantly ask, scared that my question may cut his story short.

"I've been thinking of home-schooling Palesa. She refuses to speak a word of Xhosa and I know it is the influence of that school."

"Oh," I say, my bubble bursting instantly. Not this topic again.

"They were so joyful, those kids. But, you know, I couldn't shake the feeling that they were only happy because they didn't know. Don't get me wrong, the school is remarkable, it really is. I think it is like one

of the top hundred primary schools in the country. The opportunities those children get at that school are endless. And just by looking at Palesa, you can just see that she is such an inspired little girl with so much to offer the world. Compared to other children her age in the township, who go to black schools, she is miles ahead. And she is just so happy, you know. But, I can't shake a certain feeling."

I am now sorry that I have allowed this man to speak to me.

"Perhaps it is me," he continues. "Maybe I do not know what I want. Or what I want for her. I just got so confused as I stood there at the edge of that playground, because I knew that they were happy and I was happy that they were, but listening to all those little black faces yelping away in English, unaware that they have a beautiful language at home that they will one day long for, just broke my heart." He looks at me. The dimples are still there and he's still smiling, but I can see in his eyes that there is a grave heaviness he feels inside.

I look away. I do not know what to say to this man and I hope that he will stop talking soon.

"Standing at the edge of that playground, I watched little spots of amber and auburn become less of what Africa dreamed of and more of what Europe thought we ought to be. Standing at the edge of that playground I saw tiny pieces of America, born on African soil. I saw a dark-skinned people refusing to be associated

with the red soil, the mud huts and the glistening stone beads that they once loved."

The train suddenly comes to a stop as he finishes that last sentence. Mphe Batho Station, the end of the line. We have finally arrived. I have never been so glad to be back. I pick up my bags and quickly get out. I do not say a word to the man, not even goodbye, not even to the little girl. No, I get out and walk home as fast as I can.

I have come to realise that many things are seldom as they seem. Sometimes what you think is your greatest obstacle turns out to be the least, and what you thought would be easy enough to conquer troubles you still.

I do not know how to make it pretty. I do not know how to mask it. It is not a piece of literary genius. It is the story of our lives. It is our story, told in our own words as we feel it every day. It is boring. It is plain. It is overdone and definitely not newsworthy. But it is the story we have to tell.

European Union
Literary Award

Rules

The European Union Literary Award is presented annually by Jacana Media and the European Union to a first, unpublished novel by a South African. Submissions must be received by 30 September. The winner of the EU Literary Award will be announced at a ceremony in Johannesburg the following March. The winner will receive R25 000 and will have his or her novel published by Jacana Media. This award is open to South African writers resident in South Africa.

What to submit:

A first, unpublished work of fiction in English (translations into English from other languages are permitted only if the work has never been published in any language).

A manuscript of between 60 000 and 100 000 words in length.

Two securely bound, typed A4 copies (1.5 space, 12 point font).

A separate one-page summary of the manuscript.

A separate one-page biography of the author with all contact details including telephone numbers and email address.

The author's name should not appear anywhere on the manuscript.

What not to submit:
Memoirs, Short stories, History, Geography or other non-fiction books will not be considered. No drafts will be considered. Entrants are strongly advised to ensure that manuscripts are submitted in their final, publishable form. Published novelists may not enter this competition, even under pseudonyms. However, published authors of short stories, plays or poetry may enter their first novels.

Send to:
Jacana Media
EU Literary Award
PO Box 2004
Houghton
2041

No late manuscripts will be accepted.
No emailed entries will be accepted.
Manuscripts will not be returned.

The jury's decision will be final. No correspondence will be entered into.

For further information:
Visit www.jacana.co.za or email euaward@jacana.co.za

**Previous winners of the
European Union Literary Award,
all available in Jacana paperback**

The Silent Minaret
by Ishtiyaq Shukri

Bitches' Brew
by Fred Khumalo

Ice in the Lungs
by Gerald Kraak

Other fiction titles by Jacana

Beginnings of a Dream
by Zachariah Rapola

How We Buried Puso
by Morabo Morejele

Miss Kwa Kwa
by Stephen Simm

Six Fang Marks and a Tetanus Shot
by Richard de Nooy

Song of the Atman
by Ronnie Govender